P9-COO-482

McGonigle Scores!

McGONIGLE SCORES!

Leslie McFarlane

Edited by Brian McFarlane

KEY PORTER BOOKS

Library and Archives Canada Cataloguing in Publication

McFarlane, Leslie, 1902–1977
    McGonigle scores! / Leslie McFarlane.

ISBN 1-55263-834-0

I. Title.
PS8525.F4M33 2006   JC813'.54   C2006-902518-5

The Canada Council   Le Conseil des Arts
for the Arts   du Canada
since 1957   depuis 1957

ONTARIO ARTS COUNCIL
CONSEIL DES ARTS DE L'ONTARIO

The publisher gratefully acknowledges the support of the Canada Council for the Arts and the Ontario Arts Council for its publishing program. We acknowledge the support of the Government of Ontario through the Ontario Media Development Corporation's Ontario Book Initiative.

We acknowledge the financial support of the Government of Canada through the Book Publishing Industry Development Program (BPIDP) for our publishing activities.

The author wishes to acknowledge the assistance of a grant from the Canada Council for the Arts in the preparation of this book.

Key Porter Books Limited
Six Adelaide Street East, Tenth Floor
Toronto, Ontario
Canada M5C 1H6

www.keyporter.com

Text design: Marijke Friesen
Electronic formatting: Jean Lightfoot Peters

Printed and bound in Canada

06 07 08 09 10 5 4 3 2 1

To my son Brian,
who used to get up at six-thirty for hockey practice.

Contents

Foreword 9

1   The Ambassador of Goodwill 13

2   The Natural 20

3   On the Carpet 28

4   One Up for Blackjack Snead 36

5   Emma Dinwoodie 45

6   Bobo Faces a Crisis 59

7   Mr. Snead Checks In 73

8   Slewfoot Shannon Gets a Brother 85

9   Uncle Wilmer Listens to Reason 94

10 McGonigle Incognito 100

11 News for Mr. Snead 111

12 Mrs. Beckett Is Firm 121

13 Snead Makes a Deal 130

14 The "Nomdayploom" Backfires 138

15 Maybelle's Buttons 148

16 No Help from Dooley 160

17 Mr. Wildgoose Returns a Favour 172

18 The Abduction of Unbeatable Bates 181

19 The Unbeatable Finds Spiritual Help 193

20 The Unbeatable Reports for Duty 204

21 The Great Old-timers' Game 214

22 "They Never Come Back" 224

23 The Long Twenty Minutes 234

24 Business Methods in Showshoe Lake 241

25 McGonigle's Farewell 248

Foreword

In 1920, Sudbury, Ontario, was a brawling railroad centre and mining town in the middle of a region that produced more nickel than anywhere else on earth.

My father, Leslie McFarlane, was a rookie reporter for the *Sudbury Star* in those days, flying about town like a small comet, from office to police court to town hall to fire hall to police station and always — to the hockey rink.

My father, barely out of his teens, had no intention of making newspaper journalism a career, no burning desire to become an editor or publisher or owner. He aspired to become an author, like a fellow reporter he encountered from time to time, a chap who toiled for the *Toronto Star* named Ernest Hemingway.

But newspaper work, especially for the *Sudbury Star*, left practically no time — even for an energetic small comet — for after-hours ventures into creative literature. But by staying awake until two or three o'clock in the morning, he did manage to write a few short stories and, to his surprise, sold most of them to the *Star Weekly*.

He once told me the payment he received for the first story he sold was ten dollars.

When his editor at the *Sudbury Star*, a demanding, intim-idating man named Mason, assigned my dad to the hockey beat one winter, the aspiring author soon learned that Sudbury, like most northern towns, was about to surrender to a state of complete lunacy for the next four months.

On a night before a big game, fans would huddle outside the arena some ten, twelve, fifteen hours before the ticket office opened. They would congregate in a long line, stamping their booted feet, pulling food and bottles of booze from inside the pockets of their overcoats and parkas, reading newspapers to pass the time, chatting with others about the strengths and weaknesses of the teams involved. Some would come armed with a bag full of rotten fruit with the expecta-tion that the referee — an out-of-towner — would surely blow a close call and would therefore earn himself a "shower."

Fans would build huge bonfires along the street to warm themselves. The city fire department seldom intervened, even when gusts of wind sent sparks soaring in the air and threat-ened to burn the arena to the ground.

Back then, fans demanded — and got — a full play-by-play account of the match in the *Sudbury Star* the following day. When games were played out of town, some rookie reporter with a passing knowledge of hockey was assigned to travel to the game and dictate an account of the action back to the home city. That became my father's job. Movies and curling matches in Sudbury would be interrupted when my father's latest updates arrived from archrival Sault Ste. Marie, to be read to the hockey enthusiasts lolling in theatre seats or skidding rocks along the ice at the curling rink. Hundreds of fans would hang on his words. He was a pioneer broadcaster without a microphone. And his fee was five dollars a game.

Les McFarlane knew his hockey. So it was not surprising that he began to write hockey fiction. Late at night, hunkered over his old Underwood, he would dash off stories, short and long, about hockey heroes in Canada's Northland.

His hockey yarns would be published by the pulp magazines of the day. Growing up, I read all of his published works. Like most kids, I especially enjoyed the many Hardy Boys books he wrote under the pen name Franklin W. Dixon — for a flat fee of a hundred dollars.

But I devoured his hockey stories. And I enjoy them still because they take the reader back to an era when scouts roamed the boondocks looking for talent, when sixty-minute men were common, when teams had one goalie who played without a mask, when natural ice turned to slush in the spring, when goal judges stood out on the ice behind the net and waved a hankie to signal a score.

He wrote during an era when fans of the game could get a monthly dose of hockey excitement through the pulps. They'd be captivated by the adventures of young men who showed grit and dogged determination on ice, battling through adversity, striving to make a name for themselves in the game they loved.

Here's a challenge. Bet you won't get very far into *McGonigle Scores!* before you start to grin. That'll be followed by a chuckle with many more to follow.

Perhaps that's why the late Ted Reeve, one of Canada's foremost sports columnists and humourist, called *McGonigle Scores!* "the finest piece of hockey fiction" he'd ever read.

But look. The audience has assembled for the Father and Son's hockey banquet. The guest speaker, a former NHL star from a previous decade, lurches to his feet, taps the microphone with a fat finger and launches into his address.

Hurry! Go to chapter one. You won't want to miss this!

Over to you, Skates.

— Brian McFarlane

1

The Ambassador of Goodwill

"It's been ten years since I hung up my skates," Daniel J. McGonigle told his audience at the Father and Son's Banquet, "but as a hockey scout I'm proud and happy to be still playing a part in the greatest game in the world."

Big, pudgy and balding, two hundred and ten pounds of amiable flab, he beamed at the fifty well-scrubbed little boys and their fathers. They beamed back at the great Skates McGonigle, former defenceman of the Blueshirts, now famed in the boondocks as roving scout and ambassador of goodwill for his old club.

"When I go to a game nowadays," he resumed, "I'll admit I often find myself wishing I could be out there on the ice again. But old Father Time catches up with us all. So now I do the next best thing, which is to try and help the young fellows coming up. And whenever I can do that, I figure I'm paying off part of a debt I owe to hockey. It was always mighty good to me."

The fathers and sons applauded this acknowledgement. McGonigle took a swig of water and tried to look as if he relished the stuff.

This was on a winter evening in one of the small Ontario places, in the days before hockey became Big Business, back in the times when every little town had its own rink and when the kids played for fun instead of contracts. When you heard the big-league games on radio and tried to imagine what the players looked like. When a visit from a famous hockey star in the flesh, even one from another decade, was an event.

"Like I just said," continued McGonigle, "hockey is the greatest game in the world. And when you play that game, remember this! You're part of a team. Don't try to be the whole show. Don't try to be a star. You do right by the game and it will do right by you. Because I can tell you there isn't anything better than hockey for building character."

The speech had been written for McGonigle by a young fellow in the Blueshirts' office and he had delivered it so many times that the lines came easily. But he always felt a little uncomfortable when he reached the part about building character because sometimes, not always but often enough, he sensed that it set a few of the fathers to remembering things about the McGonigle career. Even now he detected an exchange of glances between a couple of citizens at the end of the table.

So what if they did recall the time he had been suspended from the old Maroons for breaking training? Hadn't everyone? What if they did remember the front-page stories after the great brawl in the lobby of the King Edward? And the time he got clipped in the Chicago crap game and had to be ransomed by the club before he could dress for the first game of the playoffs? That was away back. This was now.

"I didn't come here tonight to feed you lads a lot of advice," he said with a disarming grin. "You get enough of that from your parents and teachers."

Applause from the small boys. They nudged each other. Tolerant smiles from the fathers.

"But if you want to be a good hockey player," said McGonigle, "the first thing you've got to remember is to stay in condition. And that means eating lots of good, nourishing food." He paused, waited. Then: "Maybe you don't like spinach."

Groans and grimaces.

McGonigle punched the air with a stubby finger.

"So what?" he demanded. "Eat it anyway. I never liked it much either when I was growing up. But when I went to training camp my first year I ate spinach and learned to like it, because old Billy O'Dell — he was our trainer, God bless him — old Billy O'Dell said if we didn't eat spinach with our meat and potatoes, we'd get it for dessert. So we ate it, and it was good for us. Full of iron."

McGonigle paused again to give them time to consider the horrors of a regime that included spinach for dessert.

"And milk," he said. "Drink lots of milk. At training camp we drank it by the gallon." He slapped his chest. "Built me up. I still drink a quart a day. Of milk," he added.

"Smoking. You can't be a good hockey player and smoke. Bad for the wind. You all know that. But there's another reason you shouldn't smoke. It's bad for the stomach. Ruins your appetite. So you don't get the nourishment you need.

"Sleep. Plenty of rest. Early to bed and early to rise and you'll score more goals than the other guys."

Laughter. McGonigle grinned back at them.

"And always remember, fellows, it's the game that counts. Not who wins. In the words of the poet," concluded McGonigle, misquoting Grantland Rice, "when the time comes for the Great Scorer to write your name it matters not who won, but how you played the game. Fellows and fathers, thanks a lot for your kind attention."

He gave them a fighter's handshake and sat down to a round of applause. They liked him. He knew very well that the applause would have been louder and longer if he had been an active big-leaguer instead of an aging has-been, but when the guest speaker comes for free, even a big name from the past is not to be sneezed at.

The chairman made a little speech. He was sure McGonigle's address had been an inspiration to everyone, just as the McGonigle career had inspired fans and players alike. He thanked the Blueshirts for sending the great man to their annual banquet. He thanked the fathers and sons for their fine turnout. He thanked the absent mothers for allowing them the evening off. Then a bashful youngster shuffled forward and presented McGonigle with a ten-pound cheese, a commodity for which the town was famous. McGonigle expressed deep gratitude for the cheese and wondered what he was going to do with it. He spent most of his time on the road, and in the city he made his home with a widowed aunt who was allergic to cheese.

Absent-mindedly, he reached for a cigar in the inside pocket of his jacket, but restrained himself just in time. Bad example. Little boys now began trooping up to the head table to seek his autograph. Fathers crowded around to tell him they had once seen him play for the Blueshirts. They all mentioned the historic goal he had scored to win the Stanley Cup a long ten years back. Several invited him up to the house to meet the wife. One, winking wisely, even whispered that he had a case of beer on ice. McGonigle had a standard reply.

"Gosh I wish I could make it but I'll have to ask for a rain check. Gotta go back to the hotel, make some phone calls, grab a little shut-eye, hit the road at the crack of dawn. Like I told the kids, early to bed and early to rise. Scouting keeps a fellow on the jump."

He made his escape, climbed into his car and had his cigar going before he was around the corner. It took him less than five minutes to park in an alley behind a barber shop and slip into the back room.

"Deal me in," said McGonigle. "And somebody pour me a beer."

Two of the shirt-sleeved players were old buddies from his playing days. No matter where McGonigle went, an old buddy always turned up. Or a friend of an old buddy. And there was always a poker game somewhere.

"Now we're in business," said one of the old buddies. "The great McGonigle is with us."

They had kept a place for him. McGonigle sat down and relaxed with a gusty sigh. Cards flickered in the smoky light. A glass of beer appeared at his elbow. He raised it in a comradely gesture.

"Happy days," said McGonigle, contented and at home.

It was half-past six the next morning before the game broke up and McGonigle, twelve dollars richer, bone-tired, and aching for sleep, trudged into the lobby of the local hotel. The night clerk, snoozing behind the desk, woke up and gave him his key. He also handed McGonigle seven telephone slips and a scribbled message.

"Where you been, Mr. McGonigle? I've been trying to find you all over town. Long distance was trying to get you right up to midnight."

"Oh-oh!"

McGonigle looked at the phone slips. They were timed an hour apart and they requested him to call Ben Dooley.

"This Mr. Dooley, he called every hour on the hour," said the clerk. "Seemed mighty anxious to talk to you. Finally, he talked to me and told me to write down that message word for word just like he said it."

McGonigle deciphered the scrawl.

"I have been trying to get hold of you for two days; where have you been? If you get this message any time in the next week after you crawl out of wherever you have been holed up…"

"Not my wording," said the clerk.

"…report back here immediately, at once, instantly, and no fooling around. Dooley."

McGonigle groaned.

"What have I done now?" he muttered.

"What say, Mr. McGonigle?"

"Better check me out. I'll go upstairs and pack."

"That Mr. Dooley seemed pretty sore about something. He was yelling real loud when he got me to write down that message."

McGonigle, who had been looking forward to spending the morning in slumber, tore up the slips and the message, dropped them into a wastebasket, and headed for the stairs. When Ben Dooley began yelling real loud, it meant that somebody was in trouble. And this time, clearly, that somebody was Skates McGonigle.

2

The Natural

Three hundred miles away, in a Northern Ontario mining town called Snowshoe Lake, at about the time McGonigle was trudging upstairs to pack, a sleepy-eyed woman was serving a pre-dawn breakfast to her son.

"I do wish Bobo Strowger would hold his hockey practices at a Christian hour," she said. "I don't see why people have to be hauled out of bed in the middle of the night."

"Not Bobo's fault." Tim Beckett sopped up maple syrup with the last of his toast to conclude a modest meal of orange juice, porridge, half a dozen slices of bacon, and three eggs. "Can't practise in school hours. After four I've got to work for Uncle Wilmer at the store. And tonight we play Tomcat Creek."

Zonk...zonk-zonk...zonk!

Stuttering backfire, roaring engine, screeching brakes and the horn of Willie Azzeopardi's car shattered the early morning silence of Tamarac Street.

Mrs. Beckett's son leaped violently out of his chair.

"There's Willie. Gotta go."

He exploded all over the kitchen in a frantic roundup of equipment. Seventeen years old. Big for his age. All arms and legs. He struggled into his parka, scooped a uniform sweater from the back of a chair, snatched hockey gloves from the top of the breadbox, yanked a duffel bag out of a cupboard, and grabbed his hockey stick from the broom closet.

"Take your time, boy. You sure you had enough to eat?"

He looked wildly around. "My skates. Have you seen my skates?"

"Skates? Where did you leave them?"

Zonk...zonk...zonk-zonk...zonk!

"Oh golly, Willie's going to be sore. I promised I'd be ready. What did you do with my skates?"

Mrs. Beckett controlled herself with an effort.

"I didn't do anything with your skates. Are they in your room?"

A wild plunge into the bedroom. A hasty look beneath the bed.

"Mom!" he bawled. "Where did you put them?"

Zonk...zonk...zonk-zonk-zonk!

"Can't practise without my skates!" he yelled.

"Good heavens, you'd think I hid them on purpose. Are they hanging behind your bedroom door?"

"I already looked." He charged back into the kitchen, circled it at random, dove into the living room, and fell over a chair.

Zonk...zonk-zonk!

"Oh, hush up, Willie," she said and went into the bedroom. She emerged with the skates.

"Thanks, Mom. Where were they?"

"Behind your bedroom door." A peerless mother, she resisted saying "I told you so."

Zonk-zonk-zonk!

"*Okay*, Willie. I'm coming!"

The back door slammed behind him.

She went into the bedroom to tidy up. But after one look she postponed the task. The challenge was too great so early in the day.

The faces of a hundred hockey players looked back at her from the walls. Jackson, Conacher, and Primeau, the Cooks and the Bentleys, Apps, Brimsek, Clancy, some stern, some scowling, some grinning, some skating full tilt toward the camera. Some skidding in showers of ice.

"I wonder how your mothers put up with it," she said to them and went back to her kitchen. She sat down to a cup of coffee and as she drank it she wondered if there would ever be a Hockey Hall of Fame, with a monument in it.

The monument would represent a woman in a dressing gown serving breakfast to a boy at a kitchen table. It would be clear that the meal was breakfast, because the woman's eyes wouldn't be quite open and there would be an alarm clock on the table with both hands pointing straight down. Six-thirty.

And the monument would be dedicated to the women who make hockey possible. To the unsung mothers who crawl out of bed at the crack of dawn to rouse and feed their sons and send them off into the bitter cold to get their teeth knocked out.

But as she pondered this she realized it was too much to expect. The monuments, if any, would be dedicated to others less deserving. There is seldom any real justice on earth.

Outside it was fourteen degrees below zero. Lugging duffel bag, skates, and stick, Tim ploughed through the snow toward Willie Azzeopardi's car. Sound carries well on a cold morning. The shattering roar of the ancient engine was being cursed in a hundred bedrooms. Willie greeted his passenger by whacking the horn. It gave him a sense of power.

"Cut it out, Willie! I'm coming."

Willie kicked the door open. The inside handle wouldn't work and there was no outside handle.

"What kept you?"

"Nothing kept me. I had to finish my breakfast."

Tim hurled his gear on to the back seat. As he climbed in beside Willie he heard a shrill voice crying:

"Tim! Wait for me!"

Floundering through the snowdrift that blanketed the front walk of the house across the street came a bleating child. Maybelle Peever, neighbour, devoted admirer, constant shadow, had responded to *zonk-zonk-zonk* as if it had been an invitation to a party. Maybelle Peever, hockey fan, age ten, would not be left behind.

"Oh no!" groaned Willie. "Not that pest."

He tramped on the accelerator. The car lurched forward.

"Don't leave me!" screeched Maybelle.

"We've gotta take her."

"Why've we gotta take her? Why, for Pete's sake?"

"Because she'll just stand there and holler. She'll go blue in the face. I've seen her do it. It scares you. The neighbours will come running out. Her mom will blame my mom. We gotta."

The car groaned to a stop. Maybelle floundered into view.

"I wanna watch the hockey practice."

"Get in, nuisance." Tim slammed the rear door shut after she crawled in among the sticks, skates, and duffel bags. "Does your mother know?"

"I asked her last night. She said I could."

The car bounced tumultuously down Tamarac Street, charging gallantly at last night's snowdrifts.

Robert "Bobo" Strowger was one of those men, indispensable to the life of any community, who devote practically all their spare time, energies, and even cash to the cause of organized sports.

A tubby, moon-faced little man, he had been a tubby, moon-faced little boy. As a youngster he yearned to play baseball, but he couldn't hit a lick, and when he chased a fly ball he always fell flat on his face before he reached it. Then he turned to hockey, but his skating was lamentable, and when he tried to shoot he never did master the knack of lifting the puck off the ice. He begged for a trial in goal and was hastily deposed after fanning on seven shots in two minutes.

But in sports there is always work for the willing, no matter how inept on field or ice. When Bobo Strowger grew up — which was putting it strongly — summer found him umpiring games in the softball league three nights a week. Autumn found him selling raffle tickets to send the football team out of town. But winter found him in his glory as manager of the hockey club. It was then that his genius flourished as a strategist and a moulder of men.

As the players swooped across the surface of the Community Arena that morning, they knew that Bobo Strowger had risen early to be with them — so early, in fact, that they had him to thank for the fire in the dressing room stove.

It was Bobo Strowger who put them through their drill. It was Bobo whose brain ticked off every faulty pass, every aimless shot, every badly timed check. It was Bobo who added up talent and desire, subtracted skating habits and shooting average, divided the result by a player's age, multiplied it all by a mysterious element he called "stuff," and came up with his own private evaluation of a lad's potential.

In the case of Tim Beckett, as Bobo chomped on a cold cigar that morning, his brain ticked out such flawless estimates that the manager experienced a benign glow. He had tagged the boy as a natural the first day he laid eyes on him scrambling around the rink with a flock of tads in the Peewee League. And with every passing year, his first quick judgement had been confirmed.

There was the deft, stabbing poke-check to steal the puck from an opponent's stick, the incredibly fast break from a standing start, the head-up rush straight down the ice, the pass to the wing, precise, beautifully timed, neither too light nor too heavy and right on the stick. There was the deceptive shift that carried him through the defence, the pivot to snag the return pass outside the crease, the deke to pull the goalie over, the quick wrist-flip of the puck to the open corner.

"Beautiful, beautiful," he said to himself as young Beckett banged home another. Bobo leaned against the fence, watching. Just let him keep this boy for another season. A natural. A big-leaguer in the making.

"Hi, Bobo."

He clamped his teeth firmly on the cigar and looked around, without enthusiasm, at Maybelle Peever.

What a homely youngster! All buck teeth, freckles, and stringy hair. And yet, you never could tell. Another seven years, and she might be driving his players out of their minds.

"What are you doing here this hour of day?" he growled.

"Watching the practice. Tim said I could."

"Oh. Tim said you could, did he?"

Bobo Strowger resumed his contemplation of the scrimmage. Nobody puffing yet. These kids were in better shape than he thought.

"Isn't he wonderful, Bobo?"

"Who's wonderful?"

"Tim Beckett. *I* think he's wonderful."

"He's okay."

Never praise a junior to his face. Above all, never praise him to anyone else. It always gets back. And swollen head, an ailment to which juniors are prone, has ruined many a promising lad.

"He's the best player we ever had in *this* town, I bet. He ought to be playing in the NHL right now."

"Yeah, yeah. That's what *you* think."

"Somebody ought to tell them about him."

Bobo glowered at her.

"Don't ever *say* that. Don't even think it."

"Isn't he good enough?"

"Look, I'm counting on that boy to win the championship for us this year. If some big-league outfit took him away we'd be sunk."

"Don't you want him to get ahead?"

"Sure I want him to get ahead. And he will, when the time comes. But that won't be until I'm good and ready."

It dawned upon him that he had become involved in a debate on high hockey policy with a snub-nosed brat who could scarcely skate. And a girl, at that.

"Scram!" he told her.

The very thought of losing his star junior made him sweat. After thankless years of running a backwoods junior hockey club that always finished last in the obscure Mines League, on a starvation budget so small that he could hardly afford to buy sticks, Bobo had finally found reason for hope. Maybe this was the year they would do it. But not if someone snatched away his ace.

If he hadn't turned his back he would have been warned by the expression on Maybelle's freckled countenance.

Guilt!

Sheer guilt, born of the realization that she had meddled in matters beyond her ken. Because somebody *had* informed all half-dozen big-league clubs about the hockey talent awaiting discovery in Snowshoe Lake. The ink stains, in fact, were still on her fingers.

3

On the Carpet

In the Blueshirts' office, Ben Dooley was giving McGonigle a hard time.

"It's good to see you again," said Dooley. "I was beginning to wonder if there *was* a Skates McGonigle."

"Can't understand it," said McGonigle. "After I gave my speech at the Fathers and Sons' Banquet I sat around with a few of the fathers for a while, came back to the hotel, and went straight to bed. Clerk must have forgotten to give me the messages."

"I called the hotel this morning," Dooley said.

"Oh."

"The clerk told me you picked up the message at six-thirty and checked out. You must have had a very interesting session with those fathers. How much did you lose?"

"I came out twelve bucks ahead," grinned McGonigle. "What did you want to see me about, Ben?"

Dooley rummaged through some papers on his desk. McGonigle caught the eye of Miss Ginger Gillespie, absorbed in tasks at her secretarial desk. Sometimes, at this stage of an interview with Ben Dooley, she dropped an eyelid in a friendly wink, and he knew that all was well. It indicated that there was no time bomb sizzling away in the background, that he was merely being bawled out for the good of his soul and the maintenance of discipline. But this morning there was no wink.

He began casting about among his sins of omission and commission. Dooley must have raked up something.

"We had a kind of cute letter in yesterday's mail," said Dooley. "Thought you might get a kick out of it." He produced a letter written by hand on two pages of pink notepaper. Dooley read it aloud.

"'The head manager, Blueshirts Hockey Club. Dear Sir — I am writing this letter because I am a Blueshirt fan and I think you should know about a great hockey player. I think you should sign him up before somebody else gets him.'"

"Are you ribbing me, Ben?"

"Why should I rib you? Listen." Dooley resumed. "'His name is Tim Beckett, and he plays centre for the Snowshoe Lake juniors. He's seventeen years old, and all of us here think he is the best player we have ever seen. Yours truly, M. Peever, Snowshoe Lake, Ont.'"

"Some kid must have written that," said McGonigle.

"Maybe. But it sounds like a hot tip, don't you think? We have to check out these hot tips, don't we?"

"I've checked out a million of them," protested McGonigle. "Morning glories. They score sixteen goals in one game, burn up the Peewee League, and get their pictures in the paper. Then they grow up and something happens. Nobody ever hears of them again."

"Is that all you have to say about this whiz kid from Snowshoe Lake?"

"What do you want me to say, Ben? Tips like that are a dime a dozen. You want me to go look at this boy wonder just because some fan up there thinks he's good?"

"Skates, I'm going to ask you one question." Dooley walked over to a file and flipped the cards with his thumb. "How come we haven't any report on this lad?"

"I guess because I've never seen him play."

"But you're supposed to be a hockey scout, Skates," Dooley reminded him in a kindly voice.

"A fellow can't be everywhere. This place — what do you call it?"

"Snowshoe Lake."

"Must be some little four corners away off in the bush."

"You've never been there?"

"I've never even heard of the place."

Too late, McGonigle caught the warning signal in Ginger Gillespie's eye. Ben Dooley picked up a folder and opened it, happily.

"One of my many duties," crooned Dooley, "involves checking your expense accounts and travel reports from time to time. I'm not a hard man, as you know. Perhaps I'm even a careless man. Perhaps I should check a little closer than I do. Now it says here…"

He paused. McGonigle sensed the axe above his neck.

"It says here that you claim to have been in Snowshoe Lake no less than twice within the past year. Last March and the previous December."

"Oh," said McGonigle. "You mean *that* Snowshoe Lake? East of the Porcupine gold camp. I thought you were talking about *southern* Ontario."

"That's the place. The one you said you never heard of. And after your two visits — alleged visits, I should say — you reported as follows, and I quote, 'No hockey talent of any interest.'"

Dooley slapped the folder on to his desk.

"Okay, buster," he challenged. "What have you got to say to *that*?"

There are times when the only possible defence lies in a frank, manly confession of error. This, McGonigle realized, was one of those times. Dooley had him over a barrel. McGonigle scratched the back of his neck, grinned cautiously and looked his boss in the eye.

"Aw hell, Ben, you've been out on the road yourself. You know how it is."

"You're darn right I know how it is. That's why they made me general manager around here. Because I know all the tricks. Okay, where were you when you were supposed to be in Snowshoe Lake?"

"Ben, how can I remember? Mind you, I *could* have been in Snowshoe Lake, but if I wasn't I must have been working — watching a hockey club *somewhere*. I mean, when I'm on the road I don't waste my time..."

"You were holed up in a poker game somewhere, like last night, that's where you were," roared Dooley. "Timmins, Kirkland Lake, Sudbury — who knows? And all the time there was a whizz-bang hockey player growing up in Snowshoe Lake and we don't hear about him until now."

"Ben, if the kid was any good I'd have heard of him," said McGonigle. "Somebody would have tipped me off. After all, I've got friends up north."

"So have I," said Dooley. "And apparently you haven't the right kind of friends. After I read this letter I took the trouble to make a few phone calls to the North Country. And what I am told, Mr. McGonigle, is that this Beckett boy is a comer. They've been hiding him."

"Well, in that case, maybe I'd better go and have a look at him."

"The only trouble with that idea is that you may be too late. Because somebody else is going up there to scout the boy too. And I'll give you one guess."

"Not Blackjack Snead?"

"Who else?"

"Oh-oh!" said McGonigle.

"You may well say 'oh-oh'," observed Dooley with some bitterness. "Because my experience has been that when you tangle with Blackjack Snead you always seem to come out on the short end."

"Not always, Ben."

"There was the case of Alex Givney."

"Aw come off it, Ben. That's ancient history. Don't you ever forget anything?"

"I wish I could forget that one. But Alex Givney won't let me. The records keep reminding me. Here it is only November and already he's fourth-highest goal-getter in the league. And last season he won the rookie award." Ben Dooley shook his head sadly. "Every time I think of Alex Givney I could break down and cry."

"We can't sign 'em all, Ben. You've said so yourself."

"But we *could* have signed Givney, dammit!" yelped Dooley. "And we *should* have signed him. That's what hurts. Givney's own father begged me to sign the boy. 'All my life,' he told me, 'I've dreamed of having my son play for the Blueshirts.' So I send you out to Manitoba to scout young Givney and what do you do? You turn in a bum report on him. Too light, you say. Can't skate. No backhand shot. This is the report you turn in on the guy who is now fourth in the scoring list."

"An honest report," said McGonigle, "on the player I saw."

"But the wrong player!" howled Dooley. "The wrong Givney. Alex Givney's *cousin* you looked at. And why? Because you went to the wrong rink and the wrong game."

"I've told you a dozen times it was the taxi driver…"

"And who paid the taxi driver to take you to the wrong rink so you'd scout the wrong Givney?"

"Okay, okay. Don't remind me."

"You *need* to be reminded. The guy who suckered you into giving up on the wrong Givney and has been laughing himself sick ever since was Blackjack Snead, a name you should never be allowed to forget. And who turned in a good report on the right Givney? Who signed him for the Bears? Need I say?"

"Look, Ben, did you call me in off the road just to blast me for something that happened two years ago?"

"And then there was Choo-choo Schultz. He has developed a great scoring punch, that boy. Especially against us. Remember when we had him all talked into signing with one of our farm clubs and he changed his mind? Who bungled that? You did. And who signed him? Snead."

Dooley aimed a finger at his scout.

"Blackjack Snead has the Indian sign on you and everyone knows it. He is a smart, unscrupulous operator who will stop at nothing, and everyone in hockey knows that too. You have more reason to know it than anyone else, because he's made a monkey out of you so often. And now he's on his way up there to grab off this prize you overlooked."

"Don't worry, Ben, I'll go up there and have a peek at the lad."

"You bet you're going up there." Dooley's pacing took him to the wall map. He stabbed a finger at an empty-looking space in Northern Ontario.

"There it is. You'll probably have to hire a dog team. Ginger! Find out about transportation."

"I did. There's a flight at three o'clock."

"Right to Snowshoe Lake?"

"Not exactly. But close enough. Thirty-mile bus ride." She turned to McGonigle. "You can pick up your reservation at the airport desk."

"In the meantime," said Dooley, "I'll phone Snowshoe Lake myself and tell 'em you're on your way."

"Today?"

"Today. He's playing in a junior game tonight."

"Holy smoke, Ben, this is quick."

"Didn't you hear what I said about Blackjack Snead? If he's after this kid too we've gotta be quick. And listen! If this boy turns out to be good, and you lose him — and Blackjack Snead gets him — then don't come back."

"Looks like it could be cold up there," mused McGonigle, gazing at the map. "Guess I'd better dig out my heavy underwear."

4

One Up for Blackjack Snead

When Skates McGonigle climbed out of the limousine at the airport on the outskirts of Toronto that afternoon, his heart was heavy, and there was no gleam of anticipation in his eye.

It wasn't that he disliked the North Country. As a matter of fact he had spent many convivial nights in the mining-camp cities — in Timmins and Sudbury and Kirkland Lake, even in such smaller havens as Cobalt and Haileybury — where hockey was a sacred calling, and the name of Skates McGonigle was still remembered. In this frigid land, where winter comes early and stays late, the fires of hospitality glow warm and constant. But the prospect of a thirty-mile bus ride on a winter night, a scouting trip to a godforsaken hamlet called Snowshoe Lake, and an encounter with the redoubtable Blackjack Snead held no charm for him.

Even less was he enchanted by the prospect of returning empty-handed. He had a dismal conviction that the mission was doomed before it began. If this kid Beckett was any good at all, it was a mortal cinch that Snead had him signed, sealed, and all wrapped up for delivery.

He noted that he had a good half-hour to kill before Flight 254 took off into northern skies, so he slumped into a coffee shop booth for a quick sandwich. Under the circumstances some men might have had little appetite; not so, McGonigle. The day he retired from hockey he gave up watching the scales.

"Been starving myself for fifteen years to keep the weight down," he told Dooley. "Now I'm going to do a little catching up."

He was still catching up in the coffee shop, having decided that he had time for a slab of apple pie and a double dollop of ice cream to follow the sandwich, when Blackjack Snead spotted him.

Mr. Snead was an ungainly ramshackle sort of man, extremely tall and lean, who always loped along with his head down and his arms swinging as if battling a gale. A benevolent-looking fellow who seemed to smile perpetually on the world from on high — a man who exuded goodwill and friendliness and high moral principles. Some people, at first glance, took him to be a professor on the faculty of some theological college, a professor well-beloved by the student body. Later on, when privileged to make the acquaintance of Mr. Snead, they would reflect ruefully, "How wrong can you get?"

A man of lively imagination and persuasive tongue, over the years he had acquired a scattered harem of lovelies representing just about every city in the major and minor leagues. When Blackjack Snead hit town he was never at a loss for likely phone numbers. With five hours between flights that day he had lunched agreeably uptown with a charmer named Sally, who insisted on driving him to the airport.

So it was that as he hurried to the gate for Flight 254, with Sally trotting alongside, he spied Skates McGonigle in the coffee shop, just spearing the last morsel of apple pie.

Blackjack Snead was not an evil man. Better to say that any scruples which may have burdened him when he first began beating the snowbanks for hockey talent had long since vanished. Better to say that he had a fiendish sense of humour. Better to say that, in a strange profession which puts a premium on duplicity and guile, he was bitterly regarded as the Master. One look was enough. The moment he was beyond McGonigle's line of vision he skidded to a stop.

"Babe," he said. "Take a peek. Guy sitting by himself. Second table from the door."

The babe peeked, discreetly.

"The big one with the round face? Should I recognize him?"

"Not unless you went to NHL hockey games when you were eight years old. Skates McGonigle."

"Oh!" Sally had always been good in history. "*The* Skates McGonigle?"

"There is only one. And I have the strangest feeling that he figures on taking Flight 254."

"Won't that be nice! You'll be company for each other."

"Sally." Snead lowered his voice impressively. "You must help me. There is no time to lose. If Skates McGonigle makes that flight he'll be in a position to wreck one of the biggest deals I've ever handled. Weeks of work could go down the drain. Even my job could be at stake."

"Oh come off it, Blackjack. I never know when you're kidding."

"Believe me, I mean it. Go in there and stall him. He's only got five minutes, and he'll miss the flight."

He gave her such an urgent pat that she was halfway to the coffee shop door before she could think up an objection.

"But I don't even know the guy," she wailed. "What'll I say to him?"

"Get his autograph. Give him a snow job. Don't fail me." Blackjack Snead blew her a kiss. "I'll call you when I come back." He headed toward his gate at a long-legged stride.

Sighing, she went into the coffee shop.

McGonigle was gulping his final mouthful of coffee when Sally sauntered past his table. His appreciative glance had just swept down to her ankles when he realized she had stopped, turned, and was gazing at him in timid wonder.

"Excuse me, sir," she murmured shyly.

McGonigle beamed.

"Yes, miss?"

"I hope you won't think I'm too bold, but... are you Skates McGonigle?"

The beam became a gratified grin. No one values recognition more than the man who used to get lots of it.

"That's right, miss," he admitted, dabbing at his mouth with a napkin and trying to straighten his tie at the same time.

"You are?" she cried. "Really? You really are *the* Skates McGonigle."

Overcome, she sank into the opposite seat, her blue eyes shining, her face aglow. McGonigle was reminded of a scene in a late-night movie he had watched recently in which an adopted waif saw her first Christmas tree. It had touched him deeply.

"If you only knew what this means to me!" his visitor was saying. "It just makes my day. They'll never believe me at home. They just won't believe it. Skates McGonigle! The hockey player. In person."

"Well I don't play hockey any more, of course," confessed McGonigle, "but it's certainly nice to be remembered."

It suddenly struck him that she seemed uncommonly young to belong to his generation of fans. Of course, nowadays, what they did to babes in the beauty parlours was something to behold. You never could tell.

"I was a tiny little girl, and we had just gotten our first radio when I heard you play in the Stanley Cup finals. Of course I've seen your picture dozens of times in the sport magazines, my father collects them. He and Mom think you're one of the greatest players of all time."

She was rummaging in her handbag. "I just can't go back to Winnipeg without your autograph. Otherwise, like I say, they won't believe me. They'll say I made it all up if I say I walked into a coffee shop in the airport, and who was sitting there large as life but Skates McGonigle himself. Where *is* that pencil?"

"I got a pen," said McGonigle, helpfully.

"Oh but that's so kind of you. You're sure you don't mind writing your autograph for me? And you don't think I'm a bold girl for asking? Because they won't believe me, they really won't. But if I have your autograph in your own handwriting, they'll just have to. I'm so excited. It's the first time I ever met a famous person and asked for their autograph."

A voice which seemed to emerge from the ceiling said that Flight 254 was about to leave from Gate 7.

"Now you'll need something to write on," she said, still rummaging. "I've got nothing here but an old envelope.

Wouldn't you know? It's an insult to a famous person to ask them to write their autograph on an old envelope…"

"Uh…miss…they're calling my flight, I hate to rush away…"

"*I* know!" she exclaimed. "The menu. You can write it on the menu. Then that will prove I met you here, won't it?"

Not only did she place the menu in front of him, but she moved around to sit beside him, the better to watch the autographing process.

"Don't let that flight call bug you," she advised him cheerfully. "They never leave when they say they will. Never. I used to work here, so I know."

Escape cut off, McGonigle uncapped his pen and scribbled.

"Don't get much call for my autograph any more," he said. "Sorry I've got to write in such a hurry…"

"No call for your autograph? Why, Mr. McGonigle! You must be kidding. Why, you're one of the greatest hockey players who ever lived. I'm so honoured, watching you write your name on that menu…oh look, I know you want to get away but could you, *would* you mind writing something above it? Something personal? Like 'to my friend Sally with kindly good wishes,' because that's my name. Sally. Would you do that?"

"Sure…sure," gulped McGonigle. He inscribed his good wishes to his friend Sally in handwriting that looked like the footprints of a drunken bumblebee, and tried to edge around the other side of the table. But before he could pick up his check and retrieve his hat and coat, Sally had found another menu.

"Oh please! You've been so good I hate to bother you. But I can't go back to Winnipeg without an autograph for my father. He's your biggest fan. If I've heard him say it once I've heard him say it a thousand times. 'There never was a hockey player like Skates McGonigle. The greatest!' That's what he always says about you."

"Mighty nice to hear." McGonigle grabbed the menu and scribbled again. "I'm in a kind of a hurry..."

"Aren't you going to write his name? You wrote my name on my menu. I certainly hate to bother you but it will mean so much to him if it's a personal kind of autograph."

"But I don't know his name," explained McGonigle, pen poised.

"Oh! Isn't that stupid of me! Of course you can't write his name when you don't know it, can you? It's Ladislaw."

"Ladislaw?"

"It's a Polish name. His father came from Poland. Ladislaw Wizcowski."

McGonigle used up two more menus before he achieved his admirer's name, correctly spelled. Perspiration dripped from his brow as he jammed the pen back into his pocket, swept hat and coat from the rack, mumbled amiable replies to Sally's fervent expressions of gratitude. He was halfway out the door when the cashier rapped on the counter.

"Your check, sir."

Red-faced, McGonigle slunk back and retrieved the check. He fished for his wallet.

"Isn't that a shame!" murmured Sally Wizcowski. "And you in a hurry. I could have looked after it for you. I'd have been glad to." She gazed reprovingly at the cashier. "The gentleman's in a hurry," she said. "He's liable to miss his plane."

"And it will be all my fault," replied the cashier in a voice frosted with irony. Waiting, she appraised Sally with one of those swift female glances which sweep from head to toe and find everything utterly wrong. By this time McGonigle discovered that his wallet contained nothing smaller than a twenty-dollar bill. He muttered an apology.

"Perfectly all right, sir," the cashier smiled. But she gave the bill a little snap before she put it in the drawer and counted out his change.

"...and eighty-five...two dollars...three...four...five... *and* five makes fifteen and..."

"Fourteen," said Sally.

Her timing was flawless.

"Fifteen," snapped the cashier. Shaken, she went over it again. "The check was one fifteen. Eighty-five makes two dollars. And one makes three. *And* one. *And* one. Five dollars. And three fives make twenty. Right?"

"Right," applauded Sally. "I thought you counted one of those dollar bills twice over. Sorry."

She bestowed a charming smile on the cashier and, as McGonigle stuffed the money in his pocket, she preceded him to the door, remarking cheerfully in a voice that reached every customer in the coffee shop. "Just didn't want to see you get cheated, Mr. McGonigle."

Her triumph was complete. The shattered cashier rang up a sale of $43.15 and spent the rest of the day trying to pull herself together.

As for Sally Wizcowski, after thanking McGonigle at considerable length and helpfully pointing out the wrong direction for Gate 7, she drifted off, happy with a sense of a task well done. That McGonigle was a real chump. He must have missed his flight by a good five minutes. She wondered why it was important to Blackjack Snead. One would think hockey scouts would *want* to get together. They had so much in common.

Flight 254 droned northward. Blackjack Snead, observing that Skates McGonigle was not among those present, smiled to himself and settled back for a little nap.

There wouldn't be another flight until next day. By that time McGonigle would be so far out of the picture that he might as well turn in his ticket.

Drowsing, Blackjack Snead recalled how he had spied McGonigle in the coffee shop, sized up his mission, and worked out a scheme to take him, all in a matter of ten seconds flat. Not that it was any great feat to make a monkey out of McGonigle. One did it out of sheer habit, just to keep one's hand in.

A bland smile took shape on Snead's face. "Technique," he reflected happily. He had taken McGonigle so often that now he could do it without even changing stride. It was something to know.

5

Emma Dinwoodie

It is not difficult for a person to get lost in an airport terminal. Even without Sally Wizcowski's help McGonigle might have managed it on his own. As it was, by the time he got his bearings and arrived panting at the gate he found that the plane was long gone and that he had a companion in disappointment.

This was a pretty little woman who had apparently put her faith in a taxi driver with a limited sense of direction. She was telling a uniformed attendant all about it.

"Is it my fault that I get a cabbie who can't read signs and doesn't know north from south?" she was demanding bitterly. "'Drive straight to the airport,' I tell him, and what do I get? A sightseeing tour, and all the time he's yakking away on the radio trying to find out where he is. I'd have been here half an hour ahead of time if I'd walked."

"Yes, ma'am," said the attendant.

"It's a disgrace, that's what it is. A downright shame." She caught sight of the unhappy McGonigle. "Did you miss it too?"

"Looks like it," said McGonigle.

"I got things to do," said the attendant. "Tough luck, folks. Oh well, there'll be another flight tomorrow." He moved away.

"Now there's a comforting thought," said the small woman. "Where were you heading for, sir?"

"Place called Snowshoe Lake."

"I know it well. You come from the North Country?"

"No, ma'am. I'm trying to get up there to see a hockey game."

"The old-timers' brawl?" He shook his head, blankly. "The Gold Cup. Everybody calls it the Old-timers' Game. Haven't you ever heard of it?"

"I've seen old-timers' games. They're a lot of laughs."

McGonigle had sat through his share of them. Always the same gags. The referee carrying a tin cup and wearing dark glasses. The collapsible goalposts. The player who skated the length of the ice with the puck bouncing at the end of a string tacked to his stick. The player who climbed out of the audience dressed as an old lady. The big mock fight broken up by a Keystone cop who was chased out of the rink. Oh, happy days!

"Laughs?" said the little woman. "Not in this old-timers' game. Nobody kids around in that little soiree. It's a very big deal every year up in that country. They play for a gold cup worth about two thousand bucks, and five hundred dollars prize money for the winning team."

"Amateurs?"

"No sir. That's the whole point. There was this millionaire made his money out of the Snowshoe Lake Mine, you see, and he has no use for modern hockey. Says it was more fun in the old days of the Silver Seven when a fellow could be playing for your team one night and playing against you a week later, depending on who paid him the most money. So he put up the Gold Cup. One game a year, and it's a doozer. Anything goes."

"Seems to me I've heard fellows mention it. But the game I wanted to see is being played tonight. Juniors. Now I've missed it."

She gazed at him, speculatively.

"Hockey," she said. "Do you mind telling me your name, sir?"

"McGonigle."

"Skates McGonigle?"

"That's right."

"I knew I'd seen your picture somewhere. You used to play for the Blueshirts."

"A while back."

She gazed at him in awe.

"And to think if I'd caught that plane I wouldn't have met you! Skates McGonigle! Would you do me the honour of shaking hands?"

"My pleasure." McGonigle felt a pleasant glow. Nice little woman. About forty, maybe. She didn't go much for makeup or fancy clothes, looked as if she spent a lot of time outdoors, and she shook hands like a man. She had very clear blue eyes and her face shone with admiration.

"Dinwoodie's the name," she told him. "Emma Dinwoodie."

"Mighty pleased to make your acquaintance, Miss Dinwoodie."

"Mrs.," she corrected. "And if you wonder why I remember your name so well it's because of the Stanley Cup final ten years ago last April. Remember that game?"

"I'm not likely to forget it," he grinned.

"Forty minutes overtime. And who scored the winning goal?"

"Lucky," he said. "Somebody had to score it."

"Listen to the man! The greatest goal ever scored in the history of hockey, and you tell me it was lucky. Mr. McGonigle," she said solemnly, "that goal changed my life. Yes sir, it changed my life."

"That a fact?" said McGonigle.

"It is a fact. Never forget it as long as I live. There we were, sitting by the radio. Excuse me. No, I wasn't sitting. I was walking up and down. Mr. Dinwoodie, he was sitting. He kept saying to me, 'Emma, why don't you sit down? You'll tire yourself out.' But I couldn't sit down. I was too excited. And there was Foster Hewitt on the radio and the crowd was screaming and it was all tied up two all and looked like it could go on all night, and then you picked up the long pass and let go with a twenty-footer that hit the post and glanced in. What a goal!"

"It bounced right. Mostly, they hit the post, they bounce wrong," McGonigle said.

"I'll tell you how right it bounced, and I wish you'd lay off being so modest about it. My husband and I, we had one thousand bucks riding on that game. Not that he was a betting man, mind you. We'd gamble…sure. You've got no business in the mining game if you're not willing to take a gamble once in a while. On property, that is. But betting, that's different."

"Your husband bet a thousand bucks on that game?"

She poked a finger against McGonigle's chest.

"The last thousand bucks we had in the whole wide world. In fact we didn't even *have* a thousand bucks. Closer to eight hundred. And my husband, who never bet more than ten bucks on anything in his whole life, unless maybe it was the odd poker hand, he got talked into this by a great big loudmouth in a Kirkland Lake hotel lobby. It started with a nice friendly little five-dollar bet, you see — even money with an old friend — and then this loudmouth got into it; and before you knew it there was a big fat argument with everybody calling each other nasty names and the loudmouth hollering 'Put up or shut up,' and out with a roll of bills would have choked an ox. He'd had too many beers anyway, but in a situation like that what can you do? You put up."

"Who had too many beers?" inquired McGonigle.

"The loudmouth, of course. My husband never had too many beers. But before he knows it, he has gone and bet a whole thousand bucks that he didn't have but eight hundred of. At two to one, believe it or not."

McGonigle was mildly shocked.

"Two to one! But the series was tied. And so was the game."

"Loudmouths are like that. Especially with too many beers. As my husband said later, 'You just can't turn down odds like that. It wouldn't be right.'"

"True."

"But if you hadn't scored that goal, it wouldn't have been funny. We'd have been living on beans for the rest of the winter. We'd have had to borrow from my brother-in-law if we'd ever wanted to hold our heads up in Kirkland Lake again."

"I'm glad I was able to help," said McGonigle.

"Did you ever help! You don't know the half of it. With the two grand we took off the loudmouth — and served him right I always said — we picked up four claims which the owner thought was nothing but moose pasture. Some pasture *that* turned out to be. Any moose that ate there would have wound up with gold fillings in his teeth."

"You found gold?"

"You could say we found gold — yes. No Lake Shore, mind you. No Hollinger. But who wants to be a hog? It didn't run deep, but it ran high while it lasted." She poked him in the chest again. "Mr. McGonigle, you'll be glad to know that we parlayed that overtime goal of yours into the Dinwoodie Mine."

"No!" said McGonigle.

"Yes," she insisted. "Mind you, it didn't make us million-aires. But it left us comfortable. Mr. Dinwoodie always said he was going to remember you in his will."

"Tell him to skip it. I appreciate the thought hut he doesn't owe me a thing."

"Too late. He didn't leave any will. An awful man to keep putting things off. So now it's up to me."

"What's up to you?"

"Mr. McGonigle, any fair-minded person would say I owe you something for that goal." She picked up a bulky haversack that lay at her feet and slung it over one shoulder. "You want to be in Snowshoe Lake for a hockey game tonight? Let's go."

"Go where?"

"To find a plane. I know all the bush pilots."

"But you weren't going to Snowshoe Lake, were you?"

"I was going home, to Haileybury. But I've changed my mind. I'm going to take in that hockey game at Snowshoe Lake tomorrow night, and you're coming with me. It's the least I can do."

"What I like about having a plane all to yourself," said Emma Dinwoodie, "is that a fellow has room to turn around. You can put your feet up."

McGonigle had his feet up. As they soared over the wintry Ontario landscape he was still marvelling at his companion's ability to achieve the improbable. A few fast phone calls had not only produced an aircraft equipped with skis for winter landings, and a pilot named Finnegan, but Emma had also conjured up a case of beer and a sack of bananas to stave off thirst and hunger during flight.

"It's always handy to know a few big shots," was her airy explanation. "And the mining game has big shots I can remember from days when they didn't know where the next grubstake was coming from. The man who owns this plane is in California just now, living the good life, so he won't be needing it today. An old friend. He spent a whole winter sleeping on our kitchen couch when Dinwoodie and I lived in Gowganda. Broke, at that time."

"He was?"

"All of us." She uncapped a bottle of beer. "That's the way it goes, Mr. McGonigle."

"You could call me Skates."

"It wouldn't be presuming?"

"I'd take it as a favour."

"In which case I'd be honoured if you'd call me Emma."

"A pretty name, Emma. For a very pretty woman, if you'll allow me to say so on short acquaintance."

"Hmm! You lie like a true gentleman, but at my age it's certainly music to the ear. You married, Skates?"

"I've never had that good fortune."

A speculative look came into her eyes as she regarded him over the top of the tilted bottle. McGonigle was no stranger to that look. His single state was a challenge to all of them. The married ones wanted to find you a wife, and the single ones began sizing you up.

"I imagine you've come close a few times," said Emma.

"Once," sighed McGonigle. "We were engaged. She changed her mind."

"Somebody else?"

"I introduced her to a goalkeeper. A mistake," said McGonigle.

"Everyone should get married," Emma said. "At least once. For the experience, if nothing else."

"I'm out on the road all the time. I'd make a poor husband. It wouldn't be fair to any woman." The subject had its dangers. McGonigle changed it. "The man who owns this plane must be a big shot."

"He is. But it hasn't spoiled him. Peabody by name. He's the one who put up the Gold Cup for the Old-timers' Game. Odd the way things turn out, isn't it? Dinwoodie and I did him a favour away back when. Now he's doing me a favour so I can do you a favour to pay you back for doing me a favour. It all makes for a better world."

McGonigle raised his bottle and said, "Here's to a better world."

Emma Dinwoodie drank to a better world and followed it up with a toast to Mr. Peabody, the big shot now basking in California.

"I have never had any great desire to be a big shot," she said, "although, naturally, in the mining game you're always looking for the big strike. I'll admit there are times when it would be handy to be a big shot. Take this plane, for example. Finnegan can set us down on Snowshoe Lake right in front of the hotel. No thirty-mile bus ride from the airport if you're a big shot. What's more, on that other plane, the one we missed, they wouldn't have let us fetch a case of beer on board either. Help yourself to another."

"Thanks, Emma. After I finish this banana."

"You just make yourself at home. In the meantime, I'd better fetch Finnegan a little nourishment in case he feels neglected." She picked up a couple of bottles of beer and two bananas. "This ought to hold him. Another thing you couldn't do on that other plane. They catch you feeding the pilot beer and bananas, they'd give you a parachute and throw you out."

She disappeared into Finnegan's domain up forward while McGonigle washed down half a banana with half a bottle of beer, belched gently, and wondered what he had done to deserve all this. Fortune had not smiled on him so broadly and unexpectedly in a long while. It could mean that his luck was on the turn.

When Emma Dinwoodie returned from her errand of mercy, she settled down beside him and announced that

Finnegan was happy as a clam and would set down on Snowshoe Lake in forty minutes, the Lord willing.

"Which just about gives me time to hear all about how come it's so important you've got to see this hockey game, and who's playing anyway. I've been dying of curiosity."

McGonigle told her about the letter from Snowshoe Lake, about his long feud with Blackjack Snead, and the showdown with Ben Dooley that morning.

"The trouble is," he said, "hockey is changing pretty fast. Maybe I'm getting a little out of date."

"Rubbish. If you're the only scout he's got, what does your boss expect? You can't be everywhere."

"And everywhere I go I run into old friends. And when they want to set up a little poker game or throw a little party for me, it's kind of hard to turn them down. That's why I'm always getting in wrong with Dooley. Not making excuses, mind you, but he doesn't quite understand the situation."

"So what happens when you watch this boy play tonight?"

"If he's just so-so I'll forget about him. But if he's real good, if he's a natural, I'll try to sign him up."

"What if Blackjack Snead beats you to him?"

"If he's a natural, and I lose him to Blackjack Snead," said McGonigle, "I'll be a dead duck in our front office."

"What's a natural?"

"A natural is a lad who is just naturally born to play hockey, and there is practically nothing you can do for him except give him a pair of skates and a stick. Apps was a natural. Bill Cook was a natural. And Howie Morenz, of course — he was a natural."

"This boy could be that good?"

"Could be. But it could also be he's a morning glory. If I had a dollar for every bush-league rink rat who has been touted to me as a natural and who turned out to be a morning glory, I would be in a position to retire."

"I am not an expert on flowers, but it seems to me a morning glory does not last very long."

"You catch on quick, Emma."

"How can you tell a natural from a morning glory?"

"Because it's my business. Sometimes you can be fooled, but when you see a natural out on the ice you just know. Something clicks. He does the right things without stopping to figure out why. Naturals don't come along very often. Fifty thousand kids playing hockey, maybe forty could make the NHL. Maybe a couple of them could be naturals. In a good year, that is."

"But if this Beckett boy is a natural…"

"The odds are against it. I'm betting he's a morning glory. But I don't dare count on it. That's why I've got to look at him."

"How about this fellow Blackjack Snead? From what you tell me he seems to have had the Indian sign on you for quite a while. What if he beats you to it?"

"Thanks to you, Emma, I think this is one time I've got the jump on old Blackjack."

"You don't see anything odd about the way you came to miss that other plane?"

"Odd? Why no. I was having a cup of coffee, and this girl came along and asked for my autograph."

"This happens often?"

"Not lately it doesn't."

"How did she recognize you?"

"She remembered me from seeing my picture some-where."

"A girl, you say. Young?"

"About twenty. It took me quite a while to write the autograph. She wanted it for her father, and he had one of those foreign names, kinda hard to spell it out. Then when I got out of the coffee shop, she said I was headed the wrong direction to board the plane and I wound up lost. Took me a while to get straightened out."

"You don't think it's possible this Blackjack Snead could have been taking the same flight and spotted you in the coffee shop?"

McGonigle thought it over.

"Son of a gun!" he said. "Come to think of it, if it hadn't been for that girl with the funny name I wouldn't have missed the plane."

"Skates, I have a strong notion your friend Snead has done it again."

"No friend of mine."

"That's for sure. I'm beginning to get the idea that Mr. Snead is a conniving, scheming smart aleck."

"I've got other words for him."

"The kind who goes around stealing hockey players before they are weaned."

"He does it all the time."

"He needs to be clobbered."

"I've tried," said McGonigle sadly. "It always winds up that I'm the one who gets clobbered."

"You need help," decided Emma Dinwoodie. "I think I had better give you a hand."

"It would be appreciated." McGonigle found himself in the middle of a huge yawn. "I'm sorry," he said. "It isn't the company. I was up all night."

"Poker game?"

"How did you figure that out?"

"You seem to me like a man who would enjoy a good poker game. Only card game worth a hoot, in my opinion. Trouble with most women they have no respect for poker. Always wanting to play wild-card games and idiot things like baseball and hi-lo."

His admiration for Emma Dinwoodie expanded. "You are a woman after my own heart," he told her, solemnly.

"Why don't you catch a little sleep?" she suggested. "You look bushed. But first do me the kindness to pry the cap off another bottle of beer."

McGonigle obliged.

"It'll help me concentrate," she said. "On strategy. Because that's what it's going to take."

"What kind of strategy have you got in mind?" said McGonigle.

"The strategy I have in mind is that when we get to Snowshoe Lake you're going to lie low. Nobody is going to know you're there — least of all Blackjack Snead."

Drowsy from beer and lack of slumber, McGonigle wondered how this strategy was going to be managed. And why?

He had no answers. But it was extremely pleasant to know that someone else was doing the thinking, that someone else was willing to look after his problems. A very bright woman, Emma Dinwoodie.

"Emma," he mumbled gratefully, as he dozed off, "I'll leave it all to you. I was never any good at strategy myself."

6

Bobo Faces a Crisis

"But Mr. Dooley," said Bobo Strowger into the phone, "the boy is only seventeen. Needs a lot more seasoning. I appreciate your call but I think you'd be wasting your time sending a scout up here to look at him."

"Let me be the judge of that," said Ben Dooley. "Skates McGonigle is on his way up there now."

"Okay," replied Bobo, with resignation. "There's a junior game tonight. But I may as well tell you I'll advise him against signing any C-form."

"You're not very co-operative, Mr. Strowger. Don't you want the lad to have a career?"

"Of course. When he's ready. But I have to think of my own club first."

"That's what I have to do."

"Tell me, who recommended young Beckett to you?"

"Word gets around. If he's as good as people tell me I'm surprised you've been able to hide him this long. Goodbye, Mr. Strowger."

Bobo hung up. Worried, he drummed his fingers on his desk. It was bound to happen, of course. Sooner or later the big fellows had to find out. Like Ben Dooley, he had to admit that he was surprised it hadn't happened sooner. But why all the sudden interest? Two long-distance calls in one morning; two scouts on the way; and Wilmer Kirby, president of the hockey club, had just called to say he had a telegram of inquiry from Boston.

Gloomily, he contemplated a copy of the junior schedule tacked to the wall.

In the eight years since the Community Arena had been built by public, if not popular, subscription, the loyalty of Snowshoe Lake hockey fans had been severely tested. For eight years they had nursed a wistful hope that some day, somehow, at least one of their two teams would get out of the Mines League cellar. For eight years their faith had gone without reward.

Every season began with a glow of promise. The seniors had just signed a new goalie with a formidable record of achievement in distant parishes. Both their defencemen had gone on the wagon. They had just enticed a forward of great talent from a rival club. As for the juniors, the graduates from the juvenile league were making workout goalies wish they had never been born. Last season's recruits were showing virtuosity that challenged belief. What the players lacked in weight they made up in hustle. This could well be The Year.

And every season ended in dejection and despair.

The new senior goalie arrived forty pounds overweight, played two games, and left camp in the dead of night two jumps ahead of a skip-tracer and a narrow-minded husband.

The defencemen both fell off the wagon on the afternoon of the opening game. The talented forward never did show up. The seniors would up the season with a record of two wins (one protested) and ten losses, a deficit of $284, and an action for damages instituted by the out-of-town cafe where they celebrated the final game of another inglorious winter.

As for the juniors, last year's disappointments performed more ineptly than ever. The juvenile sensations lost all their games and most of their teeth. The hustling hockey club hustled right into the basement and stayed there.

"We don't ask much," Wilmer Kirby used to tell Bobo. "We don't even expect much. But can't we hope for a team that could come second some day? Anywhere but last? Is it too much to ask?"

Apparently, it was. Golden Valley won the senior title nearly every year, with monotonous consistency. Tomcat Creek took the junior title season after season, and occasionally followed it up with the senior championship just to rub in the salt. People even began wondering out loud if Bobo Strowger was really the man to run the hockey club, after all.

And then came hope, in the person of young Tim Beckett.

Bobo watched the boy come up through the ranks, hardly able to believe the early promise would be fulfilled. Now, at seventeen, the big forward was the greatest natural hockey player who had ever dazzled the fans in the Community Arena, ready to crack the junior league wide open and avenge the humiliations of the past. This, the fans told themselves with fingers crossed, could really be The Year.

There was one tiny insect in the soothing balm. Tim Beckett, a player almost too good to be true, was certainly too good to remain long in Snowshoe Lake. Three years at most. Perhaps two. Perhaps only one — just long enough to win the junior title. Snowshoe Lake and Bobo Strowger would settle for that.

But with two scouts on the way he mightn't even get that year. The big league was getting more powerful and the amateurs, weakened by the war, were losing their old control. When professionals set their sights on a prospect, strange things could happen. Bobo decided he needed a strong ally. And what stronger ally than a boy's mother? If she took the right attitude. And why wouldn't she? He picked up the phone and called Mrs. Beckett.

"I wonder if I could drop around for a little talk," he said.

"I wish you would, Mr. Strowger. I've had a few strange phone calls today and they bother me."

"Phone calls, Mrs. Beckett? What kind of phone calls?" Surely the Blueshirts and the Bears hadn't been working on her already.

"Just people around town. But apparently there's some kind of nonsensical rumour that Tim's been asked to play for some big outfit in the city. I know it's ridiculous but my friends have been asking me about it."

"I'll be at your house in ten minutes," said Bobo, hastily.

He was there in five. She invited him into her immaculate living room and gave him a cup of tea.

"Now then," she said briskly. "What is this all about?"

"Mrs. Beckett, this rumour you heard, it isn't as crazy as you think."

"A professional team interested in Tim?"

"Two. A couple of scouts are on their way up to watch him play tonight."

"Well, that's very flattering of course. I hope it doesn't go to the boy's head. But he knows perfectly well I wouldn't let him leave home. Who told these people about Tim?"

"Mrs. Beckett, as near as I can figure there must have been some bird dogs in town."

"Bird dogs?"

"That's right. Usually I can spot them right away. Know most of them by sight. But these must have been a couple of new ones."

"What is a bird dog, Mr. Strowger?"

"He's a kind of a hockey scout. Not a real scout. But a scout *for* a scout. The pro clubs are getting so hungry for talent they have 'em all over the place nowadays. Could be a commercial traveller, a salesman, a newspaper fellow — almost anyone who knows something about hockey. It could even be a manager like me."

"Are you a bird dog, Mr. Strowger?" she asked shrewdly.

"No ma'am. I want to hang on to my players. When a bird dog flushes out a player he likes he passes along the tip to the club he's tied up with."

"And you think some of these bird dogs are interested in Tim?"

"A couple of them must have snuck into town without me knowing about it. I've had calls from two big-league clubs today. A couple of scouts are coming in to double-check. That's why I'm going to need your help because if they like the boy they'll probably try to sign him up."

"Are these scouts friends of yours?"

"No friends of mine. But they're big-time. One of them is called Blackjack Snead. He scouts for the Bears. A real operator. And the other is Skates McGonigle from the Blueshirts."

"I see. Well, Mr. Strowger," she said firmly, "if they show up at that game tonight I want you to talk to these bird dogs."

"Scouts," corrected Bobo. "The bird dog flushes the talent and then the scout moves in."

"Such gibberish. I want you to tell them that it won't do them a bit of good and that they're wasting their time."

"I'm glad to hear you say that, Mrs. Beckett. I don't want to lose the boy. We need him."

"You tell them," said Mrs. Beckett, "to go back where they came from."

"It mightn't be that simple, Mrs. Beckett. You see, it was bound to happen sooner or later. Matter of fact I'm surprised they haven't taken a gander at the kid long before this. Mind you, I've always played him down when anyone asked about him, but you can't hide a natural like Tim forever. No two ways about it; he's got a great hockey future ahead of him."

"He's got another year in high school ahead of him."

"That's right. So we've got to protect him. Mind you, most times a boy doesn't *want* protection. Most of them would give their eye teeth to have a big-league scout say hello to them, even. This fellow Blackjack Snead, for example, he works on that. Flatters them. Promises them the moon. And as for Skates McGonigle, maybe you've never heard of him, but he's a great hero to all the kids. Some of them would follow him right out of town like that pie-eyed piper in the school books."

"You think Tim would be silly enough to follow a man like that out of Snowshoe Lake?"

"No ma'am. All I'm saying is that we have to watch out for them. They'll probably come and talk to you, tell you how Tim can make a fortune playing hockey for them."

"At seventeen years of age I don't want anyone filling my boy's head with notions that he can make a fortune without working for it."

"Oh he'd have to work, all right. Big-time hockey isn't easy. And when the time comes I think he'll make it and make it big."

Mrs. Beckett folded her arms and gazed at Bobo Strowger for a full five seconds before she said, in a voice dangerously quiet: "Are you trying to tell me that you want him to turn professional?"

"When the time comes. The main thing is, don't let him sign anything. And don't let them talk *you* into signing anything either."

"You needn't worry about that, Mr. Strowger. But I'm counting on you to do your part too. If you so much as let either of those men even talk to Tim I'll simply take him right off your hockey team."

"Oh now, Mrs. Beckett, you wouldn't do a thing like that."

"Wouldn't I?"

Somehow Bobo found himself backing out of the living room and arriving at the front door.

"You'd make a talented boy like that hang up his skates?"

"For his own protection, yes." She opened the door and Bobo found himself out on the front porch.

"One of the greatest natural players I ever laid eyes on? A kid who's a cinch for the big time? You'd haul him off the team? Why, at this stage it could ruin his career."

"If you want my boy to play hockey for you, then you've got to play ball with me. Understand?" The door was closing.

"Uh. Yes, I guess I do."

"Good. Then I'll be counting on you. Thanks for coming, Mr. Strowger."

"Don't mention it. I mean, it was a pleasure. Thank you, Mrs. Beckett."

He was talking to a closed door. Bobo headed back to his car, wondering how it happened that she had put him on the defensive. But as he got behind the wheel, he experienced a feeling of relief. Even Blackjack Snead would never talk that woman into anything. Nor would Skates McGonigle. The best prospect in junior hockey was safe for this season. Snowshoe Lake would win the junior title for sure. This would be The Year.

He headed directly for the Main Street establishment of Wilmer Kirby, Prospectors' Supplies. Mr. Kirby, president of the hockey club, was Mrs. Beckett's brother. A stout, breathless man, there was no more devout hockey fan in Northern Ontario. He had once made a trip south to take in an entire Stanley Cup series.

"Take a look at this, Bobo," he said. "Another telegram."

"Another?"

"From Chicago this time. What's going on, Bobo?"

Bobo read the message. "Please advise re eligibility and status of Tim Beckett your club how do you rate him as prospect please advise collect." Bobo shook his head. "I'm hanged if I can figure it out."

"What set it all off, Bobo? There must have been *something*."

"So help me, Wilmer, I have no idea. All I can figure is that there must have been a bird dog in town."

"*One* bird dog? We're going all nice and easy and all of a sudden you begin getting phone calls and I start getting telegrams all the way from the States. And you tell me two scouts are heading this way."

"There is more to this than meets the eye," said Bobo sagely. "Must be."

"Do bird dogs travel in fours?"

"At playoff time they travel in herds," said Bobo. "Scouts *and* bird dogs come out in the open at playoff time. But they don't usually bunch up at this time of year."

"Bobo, I don't think you ought to play that boy in tonight's game."

"Oh now, wait a minute, Wilmer. There's no need of that. When those scouts show up I'm going to tell them they can look but they can't touch."

"You think they'll listen to you, Bobo?"

"They've got to listen." He told Wilmer about his interview with Tim's mother. "She's on our side. Anybody who tries to sign the boy has to talk to her. Can't sign him without her okay. And the minute they start talking, she'll throw them out."

"And haul him right off the club, like she said she would. And if she said that, Bobo, she'll do it. No sir, we can't afford to let those scouts have so much as a peek at him."

"Maybe you're right but what excuse have I got for benching him?"

Wilmer Kirby could be very stubborn.

"We've got to figure out something," he said. "We'll probably lose the game, but we're three games ahead now and we'll pick it up next time. Start thinking, Bobo."

Tim Beckett worked at his Uncle Wilmer's store on Saturdays and every afternoon after school. This afternoon he was a little late. The reason — his girl.

What with hockey, the irksome demands of grade twelve, and the part-time job at Uncle Wilmer's, he had little time for girls. Susie Howard had long ago realized that she would have to be content with whatever crumbs of attention he could spare from a busy life.

Other girls were escorted to school dances and parties by devoted boyfriends. Other girls were treated to Cokes in Davey's Place after school and to the movies on Friday nights. But not Tim Beckett's girl. Her title rested squarely on the understanding that hockey was his first love.

He took her skating on Saturday evenings, if there was nothing else going on at the rink. He carried her books after school on his way to Uncle Wilmer's — a mere two blocks and no lingering at the gate. He bestowed a nod of recognition upon her when she came to watch hockey practice. She got a goodnight kiss once in a while, for which she was properly grateful. But once, when another boy took her out, he made such an outraged fuss about it that she was flattered out of her senses.

These limited expressions of devotion were enough to keep her in a state of modified rapture. It gave her, too, a heady feeling of feminine confidence to know that her dearest friends were nibbling their fingernails with envy and waiting hopefully for the day when she would be deposed.

They had been waiting for two years now. Granted that Tim had little time for her, at least he had no time for anyone else. It was surely something to know that she had been chosen above all others, although it did make her a little uneasy to suspect that perhaps he just didn't have time to look around.

This uneasiness was allied to a haunting fear that he would be snatched away at any moment from Snowshoe Lake into the remote distances of big-time hockey. Every time she watched him play she was dismally aware that her apprehensions were well-founded and that the day was not far off.

It was not surprising, then, in view of the spate of rumours flooding Snowshoe Lake that afternoon, that when Tim emerged from school, grinned "Hi," and reached for her books, she promptly flared up and accused him of "keeping things from her." They argued all the way to her gate. Everyone in town, she said, knew that big-league scouts were trying to sign him up. Everyone in town knew that he had been offered no less than three professional contracts calling for staggering sums of money. Everyone, that is, except his own girlfriend, who might have had a reasonable right to expect that he would confide in her about matters of such moment.

The more he expostulated, the more he declared that he knew nothing about any big-league scouts or any contracts, the more he insisted that he hadn't the faintest intention of leaving Snowshoe Lake, the more she insisted that he lied in his teeth. They had a first-class row, and when finally she marched into the house and slammed the door, he was still protesting innocence and trying to discover what it was all about. Moodily, he proceeded to Uncle Wilmer's store, meditating on the contrariness of women. It would serve her right, he reflected, if a big-league scout did show up and offer him one of those fabulous contracts with a junior club where a fellow had nothing to do but play hockey all day long.

No chance of that, however. His mother said he had to finish school. Some of the fellows said the big-league clubs had a way of getting around that. They sent you to a special college where the teachers were all hockey fans with a pleasant custom of giving high marks to any good player a club sent them, no matter how stupid he might be. It didn't sound likely, but Willie Azzeopardi swore it was a fact.

He went into the store. Uncle Wilmer was engaged in earnest discussion with Bobo Strowger.

"Hi, Uncle Wilmer. Hi, Bobo," he said. "Hey, what's all this talk about scouts coming up for tonight's game? I've been hearing all kinds of rumours. What gives?"

Uncle Wilmer regarded his nephew thoughtfully.

"Scouts?"

"You haven't heard? There's nothing to it?"

Bobo gazed at the ceiling. Let Uncle Wilmer carry the ball.

"Tim," said Uncle Wilmer, rubbing his chin, "I'm going to ask you a plain and simple question, and I'd like a plain and simple answer."

"Sure."

"Have you been in touch with anybody on any of those big hockey clubs, like asking them for a tryout or anything like that?"

Tim shook his head.

"I wouldn't have the nerve."

"Wouldn't want to turn your head, but it appears like some of the big clubs have heard some nice things about you. Funny part about it is every one of them heard about you at the same time. All of a sudden-like. You got any idea how that could have happened?"

"Sure."

"How?"

"Maybelle Peever."

"Who?"

"Little kid lives across the street. She's a nut. Always hanging around the rink. Collects hockey buttons. Writes fan letters. You know who I mean."

"Maybelle Peever!" yelped Bobo. "*Now* I've got it!"

"Bugs me all the time. Sounds like something she might have done."

Bobo pounded the counter.

"Hockey practice. I should have remembered. Came sidling up to me, she did and said somebody ought to tell the big clubs about you. And when I told her 'no' she looked as guilty as if she'd just set fire to the rink."

This was the moment Maybelle Peever chose to enter the store to buy a dime's worth of nails, which her mother didn't need. With Maybelle any excuse would serve if it brought her a word from her hero. But when she stepped inside and three heads turned, three pairs of eyes glared, and Bobo Strowger bellowed, "Why, there she is now." Maybelle decided that this was no time to be buying nails. She reached for the doorknob.

Tim said, "Maybelle, I want to talk to you."

He took one step, and Maybelle uttered a screech of terror, yanked the door open and fled.

She was halfway down the steps by the time he reached the door. "Come back here, Maybelle. I just want to ask you a question."

Maybelle didn't even look back. She hit the road like a scared rabbit just as Tim hit a patch of ice at the top of the steps. In eight seasons of hockey, with their normal quota of headlong spills and dives, he had never performed a more spectacular cartwheel. He went sailing wildly into a snowbank and the back of his head hit the bottom step with an explosion of stars.

Bobo Strowger and Uncle Wilmer gaped in spellbound horror. Bobo was the first to find voice.

"Oh no!" he moaned. "There goes our hockey team."

Maybelle kept right on running.

7

Mr. Snead Checks In

All the first-aid manuals will tell you that a lad who has just done a tailspin down a flight of steps and wound up senseless in a snowbank should be left severely alone until the doctor comes.

Uncle Wilmer was not a student of first-aid manuals, but as an old Northerner he was convinced that anyone left lying around in a snowbank in five-below-zero weather is apt to catch pneumonia. When a hasty examination indicated that his nephew hadn't broken his neck he simply said to Bobo Strowger, "You grab his feet." Between them they lugged the unconscious Tim back into the store and deposited him full length on the counter. In the course of this operation Tim's head hit the cash register and rang up a "No Sale."

This had an immediately restorative effect. Tim's eyes opened, he blinked in a dazed sort of way and muttered, "Who's ringing all the bells? What happened?"

"Thank the Lord!" said Bobo, piously. And Uncle Wilmer, looking down at his nephew with a gusty sigh of relief, asked him how he felt and if he could move his head. Tim answered this by sitting up and rubbing the back of his skull.

"Wow!" he groaned. "What hit me?"

"That's what you get for chasin' girls, boy," said Uncle Wilmer, jovially. "You knocked yourself out, that's all."

"Can you move your arms?" Bobo's voice was anxious. Tim moved his arms. "Now your legs. Let me help you down off that counter."

They assisted the patient to the floor, where he stood swaying gently and complaining of a headache. Uncle Wilmer examined the back of his nephew's head and reported a lump bigger than a billiard ball.

"No bones broken, anyhow," said Bobo. "Gave me a scare. Could have broken his leg. Or his neck. Could have been out for the rest of the season."

"He's out for tonight," said Uncle Wilmer.

"What?" yelled Tim. "There's nothing wrong with me."

"Wouldn't think of letting you play tonight. It wouldn't be safe. Would it, Bobo?"

Bobo was on the point of declaring that Tim was sound as a dollar when a wink from Uncle Wilmer brought him up short.

"You could have a concussion," he agreed, suddenly realizing what the club president was up to. "Maybe we'd better not take any chances."

"But I feel fine," Tim protested. "You wouldn't keep me out of the lineup just because of a little bump on the head, would you?"

"We're responsible for your health, boy," Uncle Wilmer said. "You'd better rest up for a day or so."

"But Uncle Wilmer..."

"Don't argue with me, boy. We're merely doing what's best for you."

"Your uncle is right, Tim. I'd never forgive myself if that turned out to be a concussion."

"But we could lose the game."

This had also occurred to Bobo. But they could also lose Tim Beckett.

"We're three games up," he reminded Tim. "We'll take 'em next time. You just sit it out tonight and let that bump settle down."

"But how about the scouts?"

"What scouts?"

"It's all over town that there'll be big-league scouts at the game tonight."

"Any scouts show up here I'd want you to be at your best," said Bobo, piously. "Anyway I haven't seen any scouts around here today. You take care of that head."

The bus that made the daily thirty-mile run between the airport and Snowshoe Lake was small, weather-beaten and decrepit. Blackjack Snead was disturbed by misgivings the moment he climbed on board. His worst apprehensions were confirmed before the journey was a mile under way.

The passenger list inclined heavily toward large, noisy women burdened with shopping bags and children. The women all yelled cheerfully at each other and screamed at their offspring, who screamed back, whined, wept, fought, and wanted to go to the bathroom. The driver was a skinny youth with a wild light in his eye. Snead could understand why he seemed a little demented. The only other male was a huge, whiskery man in a coonskin coat.

The whiskery man, who apparently spent much of his time in stables and beer parlours, wedged himself companionably into the seat beside Snead. He opened up a one-sided conversation which was to go on for the entire journey.

"Vere you go, mister?" he bellowed.

"Snowshoe Lake."

"Vat you do for living, hey?"

"Salesman," replied Snead, discouragingly, and looked out the window.

"Vat you sell, hey?"

"Soap," hazarded Snead, deciding on a product in which his neighbour was unlikely to be interested.

"Vat kind of zoup you sell, hey?"

"All kinds."

"I like zoup. Any kind." From then on Snead's fragrant neighbour discoursed on soup, lumber-camp cooks he had known, the care and feeding of horses, the high price of hay, and other topics of like interest. Snead, who was by no means anti-social, might have even learned something but for the fact that his attention was distracted by the clamour of the women, the squalling of the children, and the alarming conduct of the man at the wheel.

It was bad enough that the road was narrow, splashed with unexpected patches of ice, and laid out by a surveyor with a boyish enthusiasm for roller coasters. It was bad enough that the shock absorbers of the bus had long lost their effectiveness and that Snead found himself goosed by a seat spring every time the bus hit a road bump. It was disturbing to realize that if the brakes were working at all, the driver didn't trust them and put his faith in the clutch. What really dismayed Snead was the fact that the driver insisted on piloting the bus one-handed, constantly turning around to converse with a giggling young matron seated directly behind him.

The whiskery man fished a black corncob pipe out of his pocket, stuffed it full of tobacco, lighted up, and began producing a smoke screen while he discussed the condition of the pulpwood market, which was full of iniquity and injustice, with all the money going to the wrong people. He smoked a peculiarly evil mixture of homegrown shag tobacco which appeared to annoy no one but Snead.

The bus skidded on an icy curve, bounced past a snow-shrouded boulder, and zoomed across the road as if bent on climbing a tree. Snead was hurled against the window and then bounced up against the baggage rack; as he came down he saw a truck hurtling toward him over the top of a hill. He shut his eyes and waited for the crash. Nothing happened, beyond another violent jolt that sent his head whacking against the baggage rack again. When he opened his eyes, the road was miraculously clear again, and the whiskery man was brushing the contents of the pipe out of his lap.

"One of dem Quebec cowboys," grumbled Snead's companion, indicating the maniac driver. "Everybody from Quebec drives car like he don't give a damn."

He filled the pipe with another quarter pound of shag and lit up again. Shortly afterward he discovered that his coonskin coat was on fire, but by this time Snead was nearing asphyxiation and past caring.

Once, Snead tried to open the window, but he was discouraged by screams of protest from his fellow-passengers on the grounds that it was five below zero and the bus heater wasn't working. Was he trying to freeze them all to death? For the rest of the hellish miles be huddled shivering in his overcoat, gasping for breath, and sending up little prayers for deliverance, until he lapsed into a sort of coma and so arrived finally in Snowshoe Lake.

When he climbed out of the bus in front of the Lakeshore Hotel, sneezing spasmodically and aching in every bone, Snead was in what might be called a touchy mood. "This Beckett kid," he said to himself as he lugged his suitcase into the hotel, "had better be good."

The Lakeshore lobby was bleak and deserted. It contained a couple of beat-up chairs, a pinball machine, a framed photograph of Mount Assiniboine and a moose head which had lost an eye. There was also a desk and a bell, which Snead pounded without immediate result. Waiting, he had time to study a large printed poster on the wall, advertising THE SPORTS EVENT OF THE YEAR, to be held in the Snowshoe Lake Arena on the following evening. This attraction, according to the poster, was the GREAT ANNUAL OLD-TIMERS' HOCKEY GAME, and the public was urged to buy tickets early.

"Sorry to keep you waiting, mister," said the clerk, emerging from regions beyond the desk. "I heard you ring, but I had to settle a little argument in the beer parlour."

"First things first," muttered Snead, signing in. His fingers were so numb that he could scarcely hold the pen.

"Glad to have you with us, Mr. Sneap." The clerk handed over a room key attached to a large brass ring. "Number 12. Up the stairs at the end of the hall. Fine evening, isn't it?"

"You call this fine? Why it must be forty below zero."

The clerk chuckled.

"Five," he corrected. "Brisk, but not really cold."

"I nearly froze to death on my way from the airport. You say this isn't cold weather?"

"Well, Mr. Sneap, up here in the North Country the air is so dry we don't feel it."

"I feel it," Snead growled. "In fact, I think I've got a chill. Going to mix myself a drink. Have you any hot water?"

"All kinds of it, Mr. Sneap."

"Snead."

The clerk inspected the card. "Looks like you wrote down Sneap."

"When I was a tot," replied Snead, acidly, "one of the first things I learned was how to spell my name. How about the hot water?"

"Like I said, all kinds of it, Mr. Sneap. All you have to do is turn on the hot water tap in your room."

Snead grabbed his suitcase. "I don't suppose there's a phone in my room."

The clerk shook his head, gestured with his thumb toward a pay phone in the lobby.

"How about doing me a favour?" Snead said. "You know a man named Strowger? Runs the hockey club."

"Everybody knows Bobo."

"Do you think you could track him down and ask if he'd come and see me right away?"

"Sure thing. He's probably at the rink or over at Kirby's. You're not playing tomorrow night, are you?"

"Playing?"

"The Old-timers' Hockey Game?"

"Never heard of it."

"You will. And if you want to see a hockey game like you've never seen before, stick around until tomorrow night, Mr. Sneap."

Snead lugged his suitcase upstairs. His room, as he expected, was a cell, although the window was not barred, merely frosted. He was trying to get thawed out, with the help of a couple of belts of rye enriched with some tepid brown fluid from the hot water tap, when there was a knock at the door.

"Come in," bawled Snead.

Perched cross-legged on the bed clutching a blanket flung over his shoulders, he greeted Bobo Strowger with a shattering sneeze.

"God bless you," said Bobo. "My name is Strowger. We talked on the phone this morning. Nice to meet you, Mr. Snead."

"Sit down and have a drink." Snead cut loose with another sneeze.

"Got a cold, old man?" Bobo inquired solicitously.

"I *am* a cold old man," growled Snead. "After an hour on that bus I feel ninety-five years of age, my blood is congealed, and I know I'll never be warm again. Mr. Strowger, how do you survive in this Arctic wilderness?"

"Well now, I'll tell you," said Bobo, pouring a modest drink, "the fact of the matter is that up in this country the air is so dry…"

"…that you don't feel the cold. Oddly enough, *I* feel it. In fact I think I'm coming down with double pneumonia." He sneezed again. "I swear if I survive this expedition to the polar ice cap I'll give up this racket and move to Bongo-Bongo."

"I'm afraid I have bad news for you, Mr. Snead. The boy you were inquiring about, young Beckett, won't be playing tonight."

"Game postponed on account of cold weather?"

"Oh no. The game is on. But the boy got hurt."

"In practice?"

"No, he fell down a flight of steps. He took an awful header. Lucky he didn't kill himself."

"If I find I have made this abominable trip for nothing," said Snead, peering out from beneath the blanket like a turtle, "I am going to feel very annoyed. Is the boy in hospital?"

"Well, no, it wasn't quite that bad."

"He didn't break his neck?"

"No, thank God but…"

"A leg?"

"Oh no. But he landed on his head, you see…"

"His head!" Greatly relieved, Snead reached out and poured himself another drink. "If he's a junior hockey player and landed on his head he *can't* be hurt. Not even if he fell out of a five-storey window. You know that as well as I do, Strowger."

"Just the same, his uncle won't let him play."

"Who's running the club? You or the kid's uncle?"

"I am. But the kid's uncle is president."

"I see," replied Snead calmly. "I guess I'd better call around and visit the boy. Cheer him up." Bobo looked unhappy. "Look, Strowger, let's put our cards on the table. You don't want me to see this kid, because you're afraid I'll sign him. He's your key man and you don't want to lose him. Right?"

Bobo sighed. Obviously Blackjack Snead was no lunkhead.

"We wouldn't stand in his way," Bobo said. "But I'll admit I'd like to keep him here."

"Okay. If the boy doesn't play tonight I'm prepared to stick around here until he *does* play. So benching him isn't going to do you any good. And if I think he's a red-hot prospect I'll sign him if I can. Let's get that understood."

"He's really not ready yet, Mr. Snead. Just a kid. He's got a lot to learn."

"From what I hear he's about the hottest thing that's hit this part of the country since the Porcupine Fire. Anyhow, I'll be the judge of that. You can't block it, Strowger. You can play it two ways. Co-operate and do yourself and your club a lot of good. Or stand in my way and get hurt. Take your choice."

"But I *want* to co-operate."

"Fine. Now then I'll tell you how I can help you. How much money did your club clear last season?"

"Are you kidding? We dropped eleven hundred bucks."

"How much did you make personally?"

"I get a small salary for managing the rink. Peanuts."

"That's what I thought. Now then, suppose you had a

little backing. Suppose we guarantee your deficit. If this boy is really professional material we might even do a little better. And suppose we put you on our payroll to run this club and look after our interests up here. How would that strike you?"

Bobo gulped.

"You mean you'd sponsor us?"

"You know amateur hockey is dying, Strowger. It's the only thing that can save it. Why don't you get in out of the rain before it's too late? This is what's happening in hockey. Big-league sponsorship. We have to do it if we want material. You have to go along with it if you want to survive."

"Maybe I'd better go and find Wilmer Kirby. He's the club president I mentioned."

"The boy's uncle."

"I think he might be interested in this proposition, Mr. Snead."

"It all depends on the boy, of course. If he isn't a top-flight prospect, there'd be no deal. I'd have to see him play."

"He might be feeling better by game time."

"I'm sure he will," said Blackjack Snead.

"There's one thing you ought to know. We've had inquiries about the lad. There's a lot of interest in him. The Blueshirts were on the phone this morning. Ben Dooley."

"So?"

"He said Skates McGonigle would be coming up to scout young Beckett."

"Not tonight he won't."

"You sure?"

"Positive. I saw McGonigle in Toronto this afternoon. At the airport. I think he was heading out West. He wasn't on the plane with me."

"That's odd. Ben Dooley said McGonigle was coming up for sure."

"Must have changed his mind."

"I'll go get Mr. Kirby."

"We could manage a couple of hundred a month for you," said Snead, nailing it down. "But I may as well tell you I don't intend to spend more than one night in this frigid flophouse. So you'd better see that Beckett gets over his headache."

"I'll see what I can do," said Bobo Strowger, and departed hastily in search of Uncle Wilmer.

8

Slewfoot Shannon Gets a Brother

The plaintive strains of "Annie Laurie," diligently, if unskilfully, extracted from a violin that appeared to be minus one string, shivered in the zero air of late afternoon. As McGonigle ploughed through the snowdrifts that threatened to overwhelm a small cabin on the outskirts of Snowshoe Lake, he welcomed this evidence of human life.

"He's home. I can hear the fiddle," panted Mrs. Dinwoodie. She hammered at the cabin door. "Open up!" she bawled. "You got company."

The violin emitted a dismal groan as "Annie Laurie" expired. The door was opened by a tall, shaggy old man who peered out at his visitors, then uttered a whoop of welcome.

"Emma!"

"Slewfoot!"

They embraced each other with joyous cries. Mrs. Dinwoodie pounded the shaggy old man on the back and called him an old doll. He pounded her on the back in return and called her a goldarn livin' daisy. They clamoured inquiries about each other's health.

"Skates McGonigle," she said, "I want you to shake hands with one of God's noblemen, my late husband's partner, Slewfoot Shannon."

"Make yourself at home," said Mr. Shannon, greeting McGonigle with a crushing handgrip. "Any friend of Emma Dinwoodie is welcome to my shack."

"Didn't you hear me?" shouted Emma. "I said Skates McGonigle."

Slewfoot Shannon suddenly stared at McGonigle with bulging eyes.

"Not *the* Skates McGonigle?"

"In person," declared Emma.

"You're coddin' me."

"It's the man himself," declared Emma.

Mr. Shannon shook hands with McGonigle all over again.

"Man alive! I heered you play hockey many's the time on the radio. You're the same one?"

"I used to play," McGonigle admitted. "A while back."

"Well sir, this is an honour." Their host snatched up a towel and fell to dusting off a lopsided wicker chair; then he dove headlong beneath a bunk.

"Deserves a celebration," he called back in a muffled voice. "Ought to be just about right by now."

He emerged with a fruit jar containing about a quart of muddy liquid and plunked it down on the table.

"I was going to open her up yesterday. But something told me to wait. 'Slewfoot,' something told me, 'give her another day. Maybe you'll have company.' And sure enough, company come." He hugged Emma again. "Sight for sore eyes," he said.

He reached for three tin cups on a shelf and returned to the table, opened the jar, regarding McGonigle with wonder. "Can't believe it. Skates McGonigle himself. Man, you was a great player in your day."

"Skates is looking for a place to stay overnight," said Emma. "You got room?"

"Welcome as a fourth ace," replied Slewfoot. He began pouring. Emma snatched one of the cups away. "None of that embalming fluid for me."

"Aw come on, girl. For old time's sake."

"I'll settle for a cup of tea. And you go easy on the specialty of the house," she advised McGonigle. "If you're not used to the stuff, it can kill you." She looked into the teapot on the back of the stove. "How many days old is this brew?"

"The tea? How should I know? I just throw in a little more hot water when she runs low."

Emma emptied the pot into a slop bucket and set about making fresh tea. Slewfoot handed McGonigle a brimming cupful of the specialty.

"You can sleep in the lower bunk," he said. "Stay as long as you want."

"Mighty good of you. I sure hate to put you to all this trouble."

"What trouble?" said Slewfoot. He raised his own cup. "Let us drink to this wonderful woman who brung you here."

McGonigle thought he detected a small cloud of bluish vapour rising from the jar. However, he drank to the wonderful woman. Tears were spurting from his eyes when she came to the rescue with a dipperful of cold water from a pail beside the door.

"One of the things I like about you, Slewfoot — one of the *many* things I like about you, I may say — is that you don't ask questions," she said. "If the Angel Gabriel popped out of that wood box you wouldn't even ask where he came from or what he wanted."

"I mind my own business," said Slewfoot.

"You'd simply tell him to hang up his trumpet and pull up a chair. If he stuck around for a week you still wouldn't ask."

"He'd tell me when he was good and ready."

"I blow in out of nowhere with Mr. McGonigle, tell you he's looking for a place to stay, and all you say is: 'Take the bottom bunk.' You're a remarkable man, Slewfoot."

"Any time you want to tell me what it's all about, I'm ready to listen."

"The fact of the matter is that Mr. McGonigle doesn't want folks to know he's in town. He is travelling incognito."

"Like a king?"

"You have grasped the idea."

"It isn't my idea," said McGonigle, uncomfortably. He had spent the final half hour of the flight trying to convince Emma that her strategy was beneath the dignity of any self-respecting scout and unlikely to work anyway. But Emma had been firm. The situation, she insisted, called for strategy of a high order.

"It is not Mr. McGonigle's idea," admitted Emma. "He does not take to the notion of travelling incognito. But I ask you, Slewfoot, when you and I go out staking ground, do we take along a brass band?"

Slewfoot shook his head.

"Me, I lay low and keep my mouth shut. Except to tell lies if anybody gets curious."

"Exactly. Now Mr. McGonigle wants to stake claim on a hockey player, but he is up against an unprincipled scamp by the name of Blackjack Snead, who has his eye on the same property and has a bad record of claim-jumping. But Mr. McGonigle," she added, with a drastic change of metaphor, "has an ace in the hole. Snead does not know Mr. McGonigle is here in Snowshoe Lake."

"Ah!" said Slewfoot.

"So that is why I have persuaded Mr. McGonigle that the smart thing to do is to travel incognito and change his name."

"What he needs is a nomdayploom," said Slewfoot.

"Any ideas?"

Slewfoot gave it profound thought. Finally he slapped the table, triumphantly.

"Smith."

Emma shook her head.

"It doesn't seem to suit him."

"I got a brother named Abner," suggested Slewfoot. "Ain't seen him in years. Anybody ask any questions I could say Mr. McGonigle is my brother Abner, come for a visit."

"I knew you'd think of something." Emma turned to McGonigle. "Slewfoot is real brainy at times. Abner Shannon. A very good name. And it makes sense."

"Look," said McGonigle, "what's the point of hiding out here and calling myself by another name when the minute I show up at the rink tonight, Snead is going to spot me right away? I know you're trying to help, but there doesn't seem to be much sense to it."

"If Emma has figured out a plan to help you," said Slewfoot, reprovingly, "you ought to go along with it. Mighty smart woman."

"Thank you, Slewfoot. And as for Snead spotting you," she told McGonigle, "naturally we've got to take steps to see that he doesn't. Which means fixing you up with a disguise."

"Aw now wait a minute, Emma. If I go around wearing false whiskers, and it ever gets into the papers…"

"It won't get into the papers. And no false whiskers will be required." She inspected some of Slewfoot's garments, hanging from nails in the cabin wall. "Now here's a nice sheepskin jacket. Can you spare it for tonight, Slewfoot?"

"Welcome to anything I've got," said Slewfoot hospitably. "Except for my heavy underwear. Only got but one suit of that."

"And here's a plaid shirt."

"You can have my fur cap," volunteered Slewfoot. He handed over a battered piece of headgear that resembled an elderly racoon that had been chewed to death by moths.

"Wonderful!" applauded Emma. "It's got earflaps, too. The very thing. Try it on, Skates."

Reluctantly, McGonigle got into the plaid shirt and the sheepskin jacket, donned the fur cap. Emma inspected him with a critical eye. She pulled down the earflaps, stood back for another look.

"Still needs something." Emma noticed a pair of Slewfoot's spectacles on a shelf.

"Need these tonight, Slewfoot?"

"Help yourself. I only use 'em for reading anyway."

"You won't be doing any reading. You're going to the hockey game with your brother and me."

She hooked the spectacles over McGonigle's ears. He protested that everything had all gone blurry but she paid no attention.

"There now," she said, standing back with the modest pride of an artist who has just put the finishing touch to a masterpiece. "What do you think, Slewfoot?"

"You sure made a big change in my brother," said Slewfoot. "I'd never reckanize him."

"What did you say?" asked McGonigle.

Emma lifted one of the earflaps.

"He said he'd never recognize you."

"Trouble is," objected McGonigle, "I can't hear for the earflaps and I can't see for the glasses."

"Don't be so fussy." She adjusted the spectacles by pulling them low on the bridge of his nose. "Look over the top of them."

"Makes a new man of you," said Slewfoot.

"I feel silly in this outfit," McGonigle muttered.

"Them's my clothes," Slewfoot reminded him. "They don't make *me* feel silly."

"Oh, I appreciate what you're both doing for me," McGonigle hastened to say. "It's just that I'm used to coming into a town in my own clothes and under my own name."

"That's why Blackjack Snead keeps putting it over on you," Emma said tartly.

"Besides, if head office finds out, or any of the sports writers, I'll never hear the end of it."

"You let one more hockey player slip through your fingers to Blackjack Snead, and you'll never hear the end of that either."

"I know it's none of my business," remarked Slewfoot, in an apologetic way, "but do you care to tell me who's the hockey player you come to look at? Young Beckett?"

McGonigle nodded. "Have you seen him play?"

"Never miss a game."

"Is he good?" asked Emma.

"Slick as bear's grease. Eye like an eagle."

"Can he skate?" McGonigle wanted to know.

"Now Mac, that's a fool question. He wouldn't be playing hockey if he couldn't skate."

"That wasn't what I meant."

"Kids up in this country," declared Slewfoot, "they learn to skate so young it's the next stage after crawling on the floor. Got to know how to skate before their mothers let them take walkin' lessons."

"I mean can he skate fast?"

"Watch that boy scoot up and down the ice, it'll make your eyeballs roll in their sockets like marbles."

"Answers your question?" said Emma.

"As a matter of fact," Slewfoot added thoughtfully, "that boy is so good that all of a sudden I begin to wonder what I'm helping *you* for. We're going to win the Cup this winter. Best hockey team we ever had, and now it looks like you want to bust it up." He turned to Mrs. Dinwoodie. "Emma, how come you talked me into this?"

"He won't break up your hockey club."

"If the boy is good, we'd like to have him on our list," said McGonigle. "But we wouldn't move him this winter."

"And if McGonigle doesn't sign him somebody else will," said Emma. "That somebody being Blackjack Snead." She regarded McGonigle with pride. "Man, you sure look different. Snead won't know you tonight not even if you walk right up and spit in his eye."

"Don't tempt me," said McGonigle.

9

Uncle Wilmer Listens to Reason

Snowshoe Lake had no local newspaper. It didn't need one. Within an hour of any happening of interest everyone in town usually knew all about it, in terms considerably more absorbing than the actual facts, which were often dull.

Informed by telephone that her boyfriend had fallen off the roof of Kirby's store and had been rushed to the mine hospital in a mangled condition, Susie did not waste time going to the hospital. Like a sensible girl she headed for Kirby's store. Only there, she knew, would she get the truth and nothing but the truth.

She was relieved but not astonished when she found Tim, sound of limb, counting axe handles in the stock room.

"Am I ever glad!" she exclaimed. "One of the girls called and said you'd hurt yourself."

Tim turned his back on her.

"Feel the top of my head."

She obliged.

"Now the back of it. Right down to my neck. Feel any bumps?"

"Should I?"

"Never mind whether you should or not. *Do* you?"

"No bumps."

"Uncle Wilmer says I've got a bump on my head the size of a billiard ball. He says I've got a concussion. Says I can't play tonight."

"Should you have a bump? Or a concussion?"

"I slipped on the steps in front of the store," he said in a disgusted voice. "I knocked myself out. If it happened in a hockey game nobody would think anything of it. Now all of a sudden Uncle Wilmer starts carrying on as if I'm a basket case."

"You look fine. Thank goodness."

"I am in perfect health. Not even a headache. The only thing I've got is a pain in the neck, which Uncle Wilmer gives me very often." Tim handed her a pad of paper and a pencil. "I'm supposed to be helping him with the stock-taking. Want to give me a hand?"

"I'd love to. What do I do?"

"Write down everything I call out. Fourteen axe handles."

"Fourteen...axe...handles." She wrote it down and then said, "Why wouldn't I write fourteen axes?"

"Because we haven't got fourteen axes. Just handles. Don't ask silly questions."

"Can't see why anyone would buy just an axe handle. If he wanted to chop wood he'd need a whole axe."

"Five sleeping bags," bawled Tim.

"Five sleeping bags. Where's Uncle Wilmer?"

"He had to go over to the hotel. Six and a half pair of snowshoes."

"Six and a half pair of snowshoes. But why won't he let you play tonight?"

"On account of my health, he tells me. And there'll be scouts at the game. Can you imagine that! Big-league scouts. Fourteen snow shovels."

"Then it *was* true about the scouts?"

"Darn right. Here I had a chance to do my stuff in front of a big man like Skates McGonigle and Uncle Wilmer says no."

"I'm glad."

"What?"

"He's afraid they'll steal you. And so am I. That's why he won't let you play. Did you say six and a half pairs of snowshoes?"

"Long ago. I'm in snow shovels now. Twelve snow shovels."

"But you *can't* have six and a half pair of snowshoes."

"Thirteen snowshoes. Six and a half pair. Uncle Wilmer is trying to hold back my career. My own uncle. You'd think he'd want to help me."

"But even a one-legged man wouldn't wear just one snowshoe."

"Here it is. Here's the other one. Seven pairs of snowshoes. My own uncle. My own flesh and blood!"

"But surely you wouldn't do this to your own nephew," said Blackjack Snead. "Your own flesh and blood."

"You make it sound like I'm trying to do the boy an injury," protested Uncle Wilmer. "He had a concussion, I tell you. Nobody should let a lad play hockey when he's got a concussion."

"Did you have him checked by a doctor?"

"No, but I saw him land on his head."

"Let's face it, Wilmer," begged Bobo. "He was only out for about half a minute. Dazed, that's all. Be fair."

"Be fair to the boy, Mr. Kirby," urged Snead. "Above all, be fair to your hockey club. That's where your duty lies. Let me freshen up that drink."

"I shouldn't be taking this stuff on an empty stomach," muttered Uncle Wilmer.

"Here you have a club that winds up every season in the hole. Year after year. Who suffers?"

"The business men who have to make up the deficit."

"Okay. Maybe they have to dig a little. But who really suffers? The fans. Because you can't afford to attract top-flight players. And the players suffer. Beat-up uniforms. Cheap hockey sticks. Cheap skates."

"Who's a cheapskate?" said Uncle Wilmer, resentfully. "We do the best we can."

"I said you can't afford the best skates. And how about tape? I'll bet one of our junior clubs uses more tape in a week than you buy for your club in a whole season."

"That's right. We're always short of tape," said Bobo.

"It costs money to run a good club. If I like the look of your club, I'm prepared to recommend that we include you in our farm system. That means we'll stake you to a little money every year to take care of your expenses. No more financial worries. No more of this business of tapping the merchants at the end of the season. Have you the right to turn down this offer? Have you consulted your club directors? What will they say when they find out you've rejected this golden opportunity?"

"I'm not turning down anything," said Uncle Wilmer. "You can watch tonight's game. You want to make us a proposition we'll listen."

"How can I judge a hockey club without your star player?"

"You have a point there, Mr. Snead," said Bobo, sagaciously. "A very definite point. I think he has a point, Wilmer."

"What's more, is it fair to young Beckett? Here is a boy who may be on the threshold of a brilliant career. I don't know. I haven't seen him play. Mind you, if he doesn't show up tonight, I'll stay right here in Snowshoe Lake until he *does* show up."

"You will?"

"Those are my orders. 'Go to Snowshoe Lake,' they told me, 'and don't come back until you've seen young Beckett play, even if it takes a month.'"

"You'd stay here that long?"

"Why not? I have nothing else to do. Pleasant little town. Comfortable hotel. I can wait."

Uncle Wilmer sighed.

"If there's got to be scouts sizing him up," he said, "I'd rather have two scouts than one. Fellow can make a better deal that way."

"True! True!" said Bobo. "You've got a point, Wilmer. Nothing like a little competition. Believe me, I was hoping Skates McGonigle would be here. But he must have changed his mind."

"Tim has always had a great admiration for Skates McGonigle."

"That I can understand," said Snead. "A wonderful player in his day. Terrific personality. Skates and I are old pals. We work for different clubs, of course, but it doesn't affect our friendship. I'm proud to say that good old Skates and I are like *that*."

Blackjack Snead held up his right hand with two fingers very close together.

"However," he added, "to be perfectly frank, I think if your nephew ever signed with the Blueshirts he would rue the day. I wouldn't like you to think I'm prejudiced but I could tell you stories about the way they treat young rookies...no, I won't say another word. After all, there is such a thing as professional ethics. So don't ask me. But McGonigle won't be here. That I know."

"What's bothering Wilmer," said Bobo, "is that he's afraid you might sign up the lad and bust up our club."

"Break up your club! Do you mean to suggest that I would even consider taking him away from here?" Snead was scandalized. "Do you think we would be stupid enough to invest money in your club and lift your best player? Gentlemen! I'm surprised. And hurt."

"You satisfied, Wilmer?" inquired Bobo.

Wilmer nodded.

"Maybe the boy is over that concussion by now. I wouldn't like to stand in his way."

"That's the way I look at it," Bobo said. "After all, what can we lose?"

"A good question," said Blackjack Snead.

He didn't bother to supply the answer.

10

McGonigle Incognito

At eight-thirty that evening the players of the two teams lined up, solemnly facing each other, at mid-ice in the Community Arena, and eight hundred spectators rose to their feet. A recorded version of "God Save the Queen" blared ponderously from an amplifier as an assurance of Snowshoe Lake's devotion (not unanimous) to the British connection. It was hastily followed by an equally ponderous rendition of "O Canada" as an assurance of kindly feelings (also not unanimous) towards the province of Quebec.

This ritual concluded, the anthems having fortified a sense of national unity by cancelling each other out, the hockey fans cut loose with a great cheer of honest relief and settled down to enjoy themselves.

There was one exception.

Skates McGonigle, engulfed in a sheepskin jacket and an enormous fur cap, peered out at the familiar scene over the rims of his borrowed spectacles and wished he hadn't come. Or, at the very least, that he had declined the aid of Mrs. Dinwoodie and her shaggy friend.

They meant well. That was the trouble. Everything they did for him came from the bigness of their hearts, inspired by a deep concern for his welfare. And there was no doubt that Mrs. Dinwoodie was a determined woman who would go to untold lengths for a friend, no matter what sufferings the friend endured in the process.

And he had suffered. The opaque spectacles and the earflaps were bad enough; he had felt like an inmate of a home for the afflicted out on leave in the care of kindly friends when Slewfoot and Emma escorted him into the rink. They knew everyone, and they introduced him to everyone they met.

"I want you to shake hands with my brother Abner," Slewfoot kept saying proudly. And brother Abner shook hands with shadowy people who kept looming up out of the fog, mumbling inane replies to pleasantries which filtered vaguely through the earflaps. Every moment of the endless journey to their seats was filled with apprehension lest someone should bawl, "You ain't anybody's brother Abner. Take off those glasses, McGonigle. Who do you think you're kidding?"

And when he peeped over the rims and spied Blackjack Snead holding court in a seat directly behind the Snowshoe Lake bench just two rows ahead the utter indignity of his position overwhelmed him.

That was how a visiting big-league scout should act. As an honoured guest. Like a king, and not an incognito king either. Sitting behind the home team bench, receiving hero-worshippers who arrived without pen or pencil to seek his autograph. Welcoming former comrades of the hockey wars, forty pounds heavier and minus their hair, who came up beaming, "Guess who?" usually trailed by the little woman and son Junior, now showing mighty prowess in the Peewee League.

And here he was, in this ridiculous outfit, skulking in a back seat, pretending to be somebody's brother, sweating lest someone should penetrate his disguise and shout it from the housetops to a guffawing world.

The players skated into position. The visitors, a scruffy but determined-looking crew, were formally known as the Wendigo Fliers, in deference to their native village of Wendigo Mine. But because a small stream in the vicinity had once been dubbed Tomcat Creek no one ever thought of calling the village anything else. It gave the post office a lot of trouble.

Slewfoot nudged McGonigle.

"There's our boy," he said.

McGonigle eyed Tim Beckett over the spectacles. There had been a great roar of welcome when the lad skated out, for warm-up. Now, at mid-ice, he waited for the faceoff. A solid-looking boy. Big for his age, McGonigle observed with relief. So often these small-town whiz kids were on the small side. Stickhandling marvels with speed to burn, but destined to be bodychecked into quivering pulp when they hit the heavy going of class A company.

"Looks as if he can take care of himself."

"That he can," declared Slewfoot. "You'll see."

The linesman stood poised for action. The referee crouched with upraised arm. The puck dropped, sticks clashed, and the game got under way.

McGonigle kept his eyes fixed on Tim, in spite of the spectacles, saw him beat the rival centre to the draw, saw him wheel and break fast right down the middle, with no wasted motion. He laid down a pass. It was a good pass, feather-light, directly on the blade. But the wingman bobbled it and threw Tim offside as he streaked inside. The whistle blew. McGonigle waited for more.

It was a good start. But the boy knew he was being watched. Blackjack Snead was up there behind the home bench. Every kid went all out when he knew there was a scout in the house. Even a bird dog. Often they went too far, showing off, hogging the puck, trying to be a one-man gang. Trouble was, the others got the bug too. They *all* wanted to prove something, all hoping and praying for that big tap on the shoulder. What happened then was for the birds.

Wait it out. Don't make up your mind until the game is over. Even then, perhaps you won't be sure. But let's see how he goes if they fall a couple of goals behind. Or get a few ahead. Let's see how he takes a hard slam into the boards — one of those jolts that sink your back teeth into your gullet.

"What do you think?" said Emma Dinwoodie, nudging him. "Isn't he a dandy?"

"He's okay," said McGonigle.

Rule one. Play it cool. Don't ever go overboard. Tell anyone you think a kid has the makings, and it'll be all over the dressing room at the next intermission. The kid gets a swelled head, and his manager gets big ideas. But after Tim's second turn of ice time, McGonigle was beginning to experience a certain glow, the sort of glow that sneaks up when you begin to realize you're watching a natural.

It was bush-league hockey, yes. The Wendigo Mine youngsters were big, rough, crude, and badly coached. Not one could carry a puck. They simply whacked it into the end zone and came roaring after it with sticks and elbows high. They played a crowding, slam-bang, knock-'em-down game against a lighter team, and it gave them a goal in the first three minutes. The Snowshoe Lake goalie was tremendous on all shots that were a foot wide of the net. On the hard ones he was all thumbs and panic. After half a dozen shots McGonigle had him tagged as a bush-league pushover.

Not that most of the other Snowshoe Lake players were much better. Bobo Strowger had done a good job with them, but, after all, with these kids hockey was a spare-time thing. One good one in twenty is a fair average. Tim Beckett was the good one.

When the lad came back for his third turn McGonigle pulled the spectacles down on his nose and watched every move. You had to consider the competition. A boy could make a thousand mistakes and still be a stand-out in this league, with its two games a week. Put him into a farm club with its hand-picked players, daily workouts, regular practices, and a seventy-five-game season and he might be lucky to get by. That's where they weed them out.

Wendigo Mine's roughshod-style of play might be just made to order for a boy with any class at all. Tim proved it right from the next faceoff, at the blue line. He snagged the puck, whipped it across to his left-winger, waited a fraction of a second, and streaked in. The return pass was bad, a foot behind him, but he reached back for it, wheeling, and flipped the puck into an upper corner of the net. The goalie, squeezing the near side, couldn't get over in time.

The light shone red, and the crowd howled with joy. Slewfoot exuberantly pounded him on the back, and Emma nudged him in the ribs.

The boy's reflexes were good. And so were the wrists. He had picked his target and fired all in one instant. A wicked shot. The puck had been a black blur.

Bobo Strowger changed lines as the Snowshoe Lake fans settled back, buzzing. Half a minute later they were groaning. The Wendigo forwards belted the puck into a corner and came charging after it. A defenceman was flattened, and there was a great scramble around the net. The Snowshoe Lake goalie leaped into the air to bat down a puck that would have whizzed a foot and a half over the bar. He dove headlong to smother the rebound and missed. The puck spun in front of the open net. A Wendigo stick flailed out from nowhere. The puck sailed into the twine and flopped to the ice.

Red light. Whistle. Moans of anguish. A lonesome cheer from a small group of Wendigo fans and a great clatter from their bench, as sticks pounded the boards. The Snowshoe Lake goalie got to his skates and fished the puck out of the cage, shaking his head.

He was shaking his head again about a minute after the second period got underway when Wendigo drew a penalty and Snowshoe Lake tried its version of a power play. Tim Beckett set up a scoring situation when he decoyed his check into a corner, laid the puck out to a waiting teammate who missed the open corner in his eagerness. The puck flew out to a Wendigo forward lurking outside the blue line.

Breakaway, with the pack in full pursuit. Tim overhauled the puck carrier at mid-ice but not in time to muzzle a desperate long shot. The Snowshoe Lake goalie came charging out of his net like a rookie shortstop playing a grounder all wrong. The puck took a bounce, hopped past him, and rolled slowly to rest a few inches over the line.

The Snowshoe Lake fans all but wept.

McGonigle was unmoved. Slewfoot assured him that Snowshoe Lake was having a bad night. The puck was not bouncing for them. Luck was against them. McGonigle resisted the temptation to remark that the goalie should take up a less demanding sport, such as checkers. The outcome of the game concerned him not at all. His whole attention was focused on Tim Beckett, and so far he was impressed. The fumbled set-up wasn't the kid's fault, and neither was the goal.

Over the spectacle rims he could see the embarrassed Bobo explaining things to Blackjack Snead before the faceoff. Bobo, he reflected, should save his breath. Snead knew the score. Bobo had a bunch of willing youngsters out there, but willingness alone is not enough. And a dreadful goalie is a dreadful goalie. The plain fact was that one top-flight player doesn't make a hockey club. McGonigle felt a little sorry for young Beckett. You can't set up plays if your wings are always out of position.

But the boy had class, no denying it. McGonigle could see that, and he knew Snead would see it too.

Along about the middle of the period the Wendigo team began running out of gas. Big and strong, they looked as if they were in good condition, but McGonigle noticed that they were lagging on the attack, that they weren't backchecking with the same bounce. And they came to the bench blowing hard.

Too many Cokes, reflected McGonigle. Too many cigarettes. No condition.

Tim Beckett began to come on strong. He beat the Wendigo centre to the draw at an offside face-off and streaked in. The goalie pulled over, hugging the post. A defenceman ploughed in to help out. Tim went around. He was in behind the net and out the other side, tucking the puck around the post while the goalie was still lunging across the cage. Red light. Jubilation.

Bobo left him out there. It made sense. The big lad was just getting into high gear. The Wendigo goalie was bawling out the rearguard, and the coach fouled up a line change; a forward sprawled belly down on the fence trying to get back to the bench at the faceoff. Tim won the draw again, hit the blue line in three big strides, let go for the back boards, and zoomed across.

McGonigle blinked. If you know your home ice you have an edge. Practise enough and you'll figure out the rebound angles. Tim's stick met the puck on the ricochet; he streaked across the cage, and backhanded the puck low between post and pad. It ripped into the twine and fell spinning. The goalie was still waiting for it when the light flashed.

Slewfoot and Emma pounded McGonigle's back so hard that they knocked the fur cap and the spectacles awry.

"Isn't he beautiful!" screamed Emma.

"What do you think of him?" bawled Slewfoot. "How do you like him, hey?" There was great tumult. A man behind them set up a deafening racket with a cowbell. Another cut loose with a moose call.

Three goals were not to be sneezed at in any company, but what impressed McGonigle was the fact that no two had been scored in the same way. Most good amateurs had a money shot, and most good goalies soon found out what it was. This lad used his head as well as his wrists.

Wendigo, still reeling from the one-two punch, began to flounder. They went back to hitting, but now they were slowing down. The hits brought penalties. Two in a row left them wide open. Bobo sent Tim's line over the fence again. This time the right-winger, unchecked, didn't bobble the pass. He fired. The goalie juggled it and dove to smother it. He missed. Tim flipped the puck over to Willie Azzeopardi, waiting in the clear.

It was easy. The open cage looked twelve feet wide. Willie potted the goal and leaped high in the air, yelping with joy. Bedlam.

That was the game. Wendigo fell apart. Once on the run they couldn't get going again. Three more goals for Snowshoe Lake in the second, four more in the third. Tim got two of the seven and a couple of assists. A five-goal, eight-point night. The figures alone were impressive even if the Wendigo team was not. But the figures didn't tell the whole story. To McGonigle the important thing, realized long before the end of the game, was that he was watching a natural.

Big. Well-conditioned. A strong skater, with easy, ice-devouring strides. Keen eyes and powerful wrists behind a shot that exploded from any angle with deadly accuracy. Split-second timing.

"What do you think?" shouted Emma against an earflap as they moved with the crowd toward the exits. "Isn't he a doozer?"

McGonigle agreed that the boy was indeed a doozer.

An instinctive athlete. The hockey talent was there. All it needed was a little sharpening. Coaching would smooth out the rough edges. Plenty of top-flight competition would do the rest.

This, McGonigle knew.

But Blackjack Snead knew it too. Of that he could be sure.

"Where now?" asked Slewfoot. "You want to go to the dressing room and talk to him?"

"Oh no."

"But Snead'll be heading there right now. He'll beat you to it."

It had taken several embarrassing lessons to teach McGonigle that Snead was not a rival to be taken lightly. Snead's next step was clear. But there was a chance, just a chance, that he mightn't take that step immediately. In the belief that he had the field to himself Snead might take his time.

"I don't want to talk to the boy," McGonigle said. "I want to talk to his folks. Where does he live?"

"Now that's what I call smart thinking," approved Emma. "They're the ones you've got to talk to."

"You can't talk to his pa," objected Slewfoot. "He's in Manitoba."

"Then we'll talk to his mother," declared Mrs. Dinwoodie. "Lead the way, Slewfoot."

Out of the surging crowd and out of the past loomed a large, red-faced man with a Wendigo ribbon pinned to his hat. He was blowing lustily on a toy horn, which he had been tooting all through the game by way of exhortation and which he went right on tooting defiantly in defeat. His eyes rested on McGonigle. They widened. He lowered the horn.

"Skates!" he bellowed in joyful astonishment. "Skates McGonigle!"

11

News for Mr. Snead

Buster McFadden had acquired about fifty pounds of lard since the good old days when he cavorted alongside McGonigle in the American League but he hadn't changed much otherwise. There was just more of him. His eyesight was good, and his memory was excellent. He came charging through the crowd, whooping happily.

"You old son-of-a-gun!" he roared, toning down his normal greeting in deference to the presence of a lady. "Skates! My old sidekick."

The old sidekick hated to do it, but he managed to stare blankly at Buster McFadden through the spectacles as a ham-like hand smote his shoulder and the horn poked him in the stomach. With great presence of mind, Slewfoot said, "You know this guy, Abner?"

McGonigle shook his head. McFadden's happy smile faded. His mouth fell open.

"I guess you made a mistake, mister," said Slewfoot. "This here is my brother Abner. Shannon's the name."

McFadden stared, bewildered and unconvinced.

"Aren't you Skates McGonigle?"

"You'll have to speak louder, mister," said Emma. "He's deaf as a post. And his name isn't Skates. It's Abner. My name's Dinwoodie. What's yours?"

"McFadden. Gosh I'm sorry, ma'am. I coulda sworn this was a fellow I used to play hockey with. Spittin' image."

Slewfoot cackled with laughter.

"Hear that, Abner?" he yelled into an earflap. "Says you look like a hockey player."

McGonigle grinned amiably.

"Can't even skate," he mumbled.

"I guess the glasses fooled me," said the crestfallen McFadden. "Sorry I busted in on you like that. But the minute I laid eyes on you...man, you're a dead ringer for a guy named McGonigle, used to play in the NHL. We was with the Cleveland Barons together in the American League. He was my roomie."

"Sorry," said McGonigle.

"Too bad your team got beat, chum," said Slewfoot. He removed the horn from McFadden's unresisting fingers and examined it genially. "But all the horn-tootin' in the world won't do no good if you ain't got the horses." He cut loose with a hearty blast and handed back the horn. "Nice tone," he said approvingly. "Better luck next time."

"Come on, boys," said Emma. "We'll be late for the beer parlour."

They pushed off through the crowd. McGonigle couldn't resist a backward look. His old roomie stood there shaking his head, utterly deflated, twiddling aimlessly with the horn. McGonigle felt guilty. It was a mean trick to play on good old Buster.

The look back was a mistake. Good old Buster became very thoughtful. By the time McGonigle and company were outside the rink, good old Buster was heading for the Wendigo dressing room.

There he found a downcast crew of players shucking off their skates and making adverse remarks about the referee. Their manager, T-bone Kowski, tried to console them with assurances that things would be different next time.

"That Beckett!" muttered the goalie. "What can you do? He could pick a knot-hole at fifty yards."

Buster McFadden drew the manager to one side.

"Did you know there was a scout out there tonight?"

"Sure, Blackjack Snead. Everybody knew it."

"And Skates McGonigle?"

"He didn't make it."

"How do you mean he didn't make it? I swear as sure as I'm a foot high I ran into him in the corridor not five minutes ago."

"Not McGonigle. I was talking to Bobo Strowger. McGonigle was supposed to be coming up for a look at Beckett. He missed his plane."

"I tell you I *know* the guy. Played with him in Cleveland. We were roomies. A whole season I was with him before he went up to the NHL."

"Did you speak to him?"

"Sure I spoke to him. Pretended he didn't know me. He was with an odd-looking dame and a kookie old geezer called Shannon. Claimed he was Shannon's brother Abner."

"Then he couldn't have been McGonigle. Buster, if a big-time scout like him came up here he wouldn't go around making out he was somebody else."

"Why not? Maybe he snook into town on the QT. He could have figured it would make the boys nervous if they knew he was looking them over. Of course, I didn't give him an argument. I said to myself, 'Okay, Skates, old boy, if that's the way you want to play it I can go along with a gag.' But he didn't fool his old sidekick, with the cheaters and the fur cap and all the rest of the get-up. Not one little bit he didn't."

"Okay, okay," said Kowski. "So your old roomie gave you the brush. What do you want me to do about it?"

"Just thought you'd be interested, that's all."

"Look Buster, any scout caught that clambake tonight he isn't going to be pounding on the door of *this* dressing room with a fistful of contracts, that's for sure." He glowered at his weary warriors. "Come on, you guys. Have your shower, and let's get out of here. Don't keep the bus waiting."

Buster McFadden wandered out, wagging his head.

"My old buddy," he muttered. "Makin' out he didn't know me. How about that?"

Next door in the Snowshoe Lake dressing room, there was the cheerful uproar that follows a win. The boys got out of their gear. Some of them were hopping about and yelping as they whacked each other with wet towels. In a pungent atmosphere of steam, sweat, and wintergreen, Ole Swanson the trainer was ministering to his battered charges with tape and Mercurochrome.

Tim Beckett, sitting on a bench in his underwear, had the good feeling he always had after a good game, win or lose. Bone-tired, but happy.

"No cuts, no busted ribs?" said Ole.

"I feel fine, Ole."

"You play good, like always. Lotsa goals."

Bobo Strowger came in with Blackjack Snead. There was a respectful silence. They all knew about Snead. That dour, lanky man who had watched the game with a poker face had the power to lift any of them out of the obscurity of the Mines League into the razzle-dazzle of Junior A and perhaps even the blazing heights above.

"Way to go, fellows," said Bobo. "You've heard of Mr. Snead, from the Bears?" They eyed Mr. Snead, hopefully.

"Nice game, boys," commented Snead. "You really came on strong in the last period. That's when it counts."

He glanced casually around the room, but paid no one the honour of a special word. Snead was too smart for that. Single out anyone, and you made the rest feel like also-rans. You could blow a team's morale right out the dressing-room window. After a while he went back into the office next door with Bobo.

"What do you know?" said Willie Azzeopardi. "I beat my brains out, and he never even asked me to sign."

"Maybe they've already got a stick boy," remarked Hammerhead Peterson.

"Ever tried walking home after a game?" grinned Willie. "Mighty long way out to your place."

Hammerhead turned to Tim. "What'll you say if he asks you? And I'm betting he does."

"He's out of his mind if he doesn't," Willie said. "Man! Five goals and three assists. What more could he want?"

Tim shrugged.

"He looks at hundreds," he said and went to the shower. Snead's casual attitude didn't disappoint him. Naturally, it would be nice to have a big-league outfit interested, but you couldn't count on it. What did disappoint him, after all the talk, was the fact that Skates McGonigle hadn't shown up. There was a man he'd like to meet. He had McGonigle's picture on the wall of his room at home. Blackjack Snead might be a big-shot scout, but where had he ever played? Five years in the minors and half a season with the Rangers. He didn't begin to stack up with a man like McGonigle, one of the great ones.

In Bobo's office, Snead was just settling down for a confidential talk when T-bone Kowski came in to pay his respects and pick up the visitors' share of the gate.

"I hope you like that Beckett kid so much that you'll take him back with you," he said to Blackjack Snead. "Not that I wish you any tough luck," he told Bobo, "but if you lose that one-man gang maybe we can win a couple."

"Ho-ho-ho! Stop dreaming, T-bone. I wouldn't part with that boy for a million dollars."

"Ho-ho-ho yourself, chum. With two scouts after him, you'll settle for the best deal you can get."

"What two scouts?" inquired Snead with interest.

"You and McGonigle, who else?"

"McGonigle didn't show," said Bobo.

"That's what you think. He was out there."

"You must be kidding," Snead said.

"Mind you, he wasn't walking around with a big sign on his back with his name on it. Buster McFadden used to play on the same club and when he went up to shake hands McGonigle said he never saw Buster before in his life. But Buster swears up and down it was his old buddy, no foolin'. He was real put out."

"Well!" said Blackjack Snead. "This is very interesting, if true."

"Buster said he was togged out in a fur cap, trying to look like a native son. Made out his name was Abner Shannon."

"There's a Shannon lives in a shack out on the edge of town," Bobo said. "An old codger. Everybody calls him Slewfoot."

"That's who was with McGonigle. Claimed McGonigle was his brother."

"I'll soon find out," said Bobo. He flung open the door to the dressing room. "Hammerhead," he shouted. "Come in here."

Dazed by this unexpected summons, and still in his underwear, Hammerhead Peterson ventured across the threshold. A teammate advised him not to sign for a cent less than ten thousand a year.

"Isn't Slewfoot Shannon your uncle?" Bobo asked him.

"Ol' Slewfoot? Sure."

"Has he got a brother named Abner?"

"That's right."

"In town?"

Hammerhead blinked.

"Uncle Abner hasn't been up this way for twenty years. He lives in Toledo, Ohio."

"Could he be visiting Slewfoot, and you wouldn't hear about it?"

"Man!" said Hammerhead. "If there's one relative he *wouldn't* visit it's Uncle Slewfoot. They haven't spoken to each other since Uncle Slewfoot gave him a hot tip on a gold mine stock that went kerboom."

"Thanks, Hammerhead."

"The stock was eighteen cents a share, and Slewfoot said it would go to forty dollars. Uncle Abner pinched my Aunt Stella's paycheque from the beauty shop to buy the stock and…"

"Thanks, Hammerhead."

"Instead of going up the stock went down. No sir, he wouldn't be up here on any visit," said Hammerhead as Bobo closed the door.

"McGonigle! Sure as guns," said Blackjack Snead.

"Buster seemed pretty sure. Guess he came up for a quiet peek at young Beckett. Like you."

"It's possible," agreed Blackjack. "But I wouldn't like it to get around. How about that, T-bone?"

"I never heard a thing," T-bone assured him. "You scouts want to play hide-and-go-seek, go ahead and play. I'm no fink."

After T-bone had departed with Wendigo's share of the night's loot, Snead said, "Now how did McGonigle slip into town? He couldn't have made it by car. And the train service…"

Bobo slapped the desk.

"Why didn't I think of it? Private aircraft came in about five o'clock. Some of the boys said Mrs. Dinwoodie was on it. She's checked in at the hotel."

"There's our answer."

"Never even dawned on me she could have brought along a passenger. But what good is it going to do him?"

"No good at all, now that I know what he's up to." Snead rubbed his hands together, with an air of quiet enjoyment. "Especially since he doesn't know that I know."

"But where is he now?"

"Right now," said Snead, "I imagine my old patsy is having a little chat with the boy's mother. Seems reasonable."

"She'll throw him out on his ear."

"A pleasant thought. Well, Bobo, let's get busy. How long will it take you to round up your club executive?"

"You told me to set a meeting for tomorrow morning."

"Under the circumstances perhaps we'd better step it up a little. Where do they usually go after a game?"

"The Lakeshore Pub."

"How about rounding them up and fetching them back here for a little meeting. Let's get everything settled."

"Good idea. Don't go away."

When Bobo departed Blackjack Snead leaned back in his chair, put his feet on the desk and smiled thoughtfully at the ceiling.

"Just like old times," he mused. "McGonigle still trying to outsmart the old master."

There was a roguish gleam in his eye. He dialed long distance and called an old buddy in Toronto.

"Hi, chum," he said. "This is Blackjack. I want you to do me a little favour."

"How little?"

"Nothing much. I want you to make a long-distance call for me."

His instructions were specific. When he concluded he hung up and smiled happily at the ceiling again.

"That should give old Skates something to worry about," he said to himself. "After all, he asked for it."

12

Mrs. Beckett Is Firm

There were mothers in Snowshoe Lake who never missed a hockey game. They would fight their way to the rink in the teeth of a blizzard. One of them, in a final stage of pregnancy, had been carried out, resisting, halfway through the third period of a tied game and wept all the way to the delivery room; afterward, her first weary question was, "Who won?"

They sat at rinkside and screamed encouragement to their offspring. A referee who incurred their disfavour risked being beaten over the head with handbags. Visiting players, without exception, were jeered as unscrupulous rascals, bereft of all sense of fair play. A hometown penalty produced howls of outrage; a hometown goal sparked delirium.

These were the mothers, with one exception, of the junior players. The exception was little Mrs. Beckett. She never went to the games, had never seen her son perform. The others took the charitable view that she must be a little daft.

"I couldn't stand it," she explained. "I wouldn't want to see him get hurt."

Entertaining her unexpected visitors that night in the living room, she served cookies and tea, and waited graciously for McGonigle to come to the point.

"Ma'am," McGonigle told her, "you don't need to worry about that lad getting hurt. If I've ever seen a boy who can take care of himself in the heavy going it's that one."

In the back of McGonigle's mind was the apprehension that any mother who shrank from watching her boy bumped and buffeted in a junior hockey game might be reluctant to expose him to the more expert violence of professional bashers. Some women were odd that way.

"Mrs. Beckett," said Emma, "if you'll allow me to say so, you're depriving yourself of a genuine treat. That boy is worth going miles to see."

"Thank you. I'm glad he played well tonight." She turned a speculative eye on McGonigle. "Have you talked with Mr. Strowger since you came to town?"

"Well, no, ma'am. I just didn't get around to it, somehow."

"In that case, I'll forgive you for coming here tonight. You see, I told Mr. Strowger that if I heard any more nonsense about professional hockey I would have to ask Tim to resign from the club."

McGonigle gulped. "You wouldn't."

"That's what Mr. Strowger said. In the very same tone of voice. But believe me, I mean exactly what I say."

"She does too," said Slewfoot. "I can tell." He regarded Mrs. Beckett with respect. "For a little bit of a thing, you speak up for yourself real perky."

McGonigle took a deep breath. He seldom had any trouble with mothers. Normally they were devout worshippers at the shrine of hockey and of a generation that made them charter members of the McGonigle fan club at that. But this one couldn't care less. She didn't even *go* to hockey games. Diplomacy, patient, tactful diplomacy would be needed here. One false step, one stupid remark and he'd find himself right out in a snowbank.

"Mrs. Beckett," he said solemnly, "I'm glad to hear your opinion. Straight from the shoulder, No beating around the bush. That's what I like."

"That's how I feel about it, Mr. McGonigle."

"I'll tell you something. When I find a promising boy, when I size him up and figure he's maybe got what it takes, I don't talk to the lad at all. Your son...I watched him play tonight, and I liked what I saw. Did I go around to the dressing room and fill him full of a lot of malarkey? I did not. Never went near him."

"I'm glad to hear that."

"First thing I want to know is how do his folks feel about it. They're the ones who've got his future at heart. They're the ones who count. That's why I came to you first."

"First?"

"Mrs. Beckett, when I watched your boy tonight, I said to myself. 'Now there is a young player with a lot of promise. He still has plenty to learn, needs good coaching, but in four or five years he could be right up there.'"

"Up where, Mr. McGonigle?"

"Why, up with the big ones. In the NHL."

"It's too bad you didn't talk to Mr. Strowger. He would have told you how I feel about this. Tim's education comes before hockey. I won't allow him to leave school and I don't want him to leave Snowshoe Lake."

"That's fine. I don't believe in letting a young fellow get all excited about a hockey career before he's ready. And, like you say, education comes first."

"Every time," interjected Slewfoot. "I remember once I wanted to quit school. Couldn't see no sense to it. But my old man said, 'Nothing doing. You'll finish the fourth grade if it kills you.' So I did. Never been sorry."

"The point is," said McGonigle, "that if he doesn't sign a card with me, some other club might put him on their list, and tie him up anyway. Then he'd have to play for them."

"He doesn't have to play for anyone."

"That's true. But in a couple of years, if he wanted to turn pro he wouldn't have any choice."

"It's a free country, Mr. McGonigle. If he does want to play professional hockey — and I won't stand in his way if that's what he really wants when he is old enough to make his own decision — he'll choose his own employer."

"But it doesn't work that way. In hockey if you're on a club's list that's where you have to go."

"In that case I wouldn't want him to have anything to do with it. Why it's like slavery. Outrageous."

"Mr. McGonigle is trying to help your boy," spoke up Mrs. Dinwoodie.

"Mr. McGonigle is trying to help his own club."

"We'd use him right. We have a good organization. With the talent he's got he's a sure bet to make it big."

"But suppose he signed, as you put it, and found that he didn't care for your club?"

"Ain't a kid in Canada wouldn't give his eye teeth to play for the Blueshirts," said Slewfoot.

"That may be. But boys aren't always good judges of what's best for them."

"We'd hope he'd want to stay with us," said McGonigle. "But if he wasn't happy we could always trade him or sell him to another club."

This remark was unfortunate. Mrs. Beckett frowned.

"Sell him?" she exclaimed. "And you tell me it isn't slavery. I never heard of such a thing."

"It's the way sport is run," McGonigle said, beginning to sweat. "Hockey, baseball, football. You make deals. If a player could go anywhere he wanted, the club with the most money would wind up with all the best ones. It would kill the game."

"So you trade and sell human beings like...like cattle. Somebody should put a stop to it."

"A hockey career can be mighty good to a fellow."

"Look what it did for McGonigle," spoke up Mrs. Dinwoodie.

Mrs. Beckett studied McGonigle from head to foot.

"What did it do for you, Mr. McGonigle?" she inquired gently.

He became uncomfortably aware of the fact that in Slewfoot's ancient plaid shirt he did not look the part of the prosperous executive.

"Well," said McGonigle, thinking it over, "it made me a good living."

"You were a star, I believe. One of the successful ones."

"You can say that again, ma'am," declared Slewfoot. "Right up there with the best." McGonigle wished Slewfoot would shut up.

"Very highly paid, I imagine?"

"I did all right."

"Tim tells me that professional hockey players earn large salaries. For how many years did you play?"

"Twelve years in the big time," McGonigle said proudly.

"You must have made a great deal of money. Did you invest it in a business of some kind? Real estate? Stocks?"

"Wish I had."

"Of course," said Mrs. Beckett, understandingly, "when you raise a family there is never very much money left over, is there? How many children do you have, Mr. McGonigle?"

"Well…uh…being on the road so much, somehow I never got around to getting married."

McGonigle began to feel like an insect impaled on a pin.

"And now you spend your time going around the country trying to find young players for your club," continued Mrs. Beckett, relentlessly. "A bird dog. Is that the term?"

"A scout, ma'am. A bird dog flushes 'em out. A scout sizes them up."

"Oh yes. Mr. Strowger explained it to me. You must travel a great deal."

"On the road all the time."

"Dear me," said Mrs. Beckett sympathetically. "Living out of a suitcase. It must be a lonely life. And you aren't very old, either."

At the moment McGonigle felt about eighty.

"Well…uh…I'm sure Tim would wind up with a lot more to show for it," he said. "Don't judge by *me*."

"I'm not judging at all," Mrs. Beckett assured him. "Would you care for another cup of tea?"

"Maybe she wasn't judging," muttered McGonigle as they walked down the snowy street to the Lakeshore, "but she sure nailed my hide to the barn door."

"Don't let it get you down," advised Emma.

"I could see her mind working." McGonigle was steeped in gloom. "She was saying to herself, 'So here's an example for my boy. A big-time hockey star, and what's he got to show for it?'"

"So what if you haven't got a million in the bank. You've done what you wanted. Think of the fun you've had."

"Fun!" sniffed McGonigle. "A flabby old guy beatin' the bushes, without even a shirt to his back."

"That's a danged good shirt," Slewfoot protested. "Cost me seven dollars right after the war."

"Makes a fellow think."

"Stop feeling sorry for yourself." Emma squeezed his arm. "To think that one itty-bitty woman could give you such a case of the dismals. You've just had a long day, that's all. A good night's sleep and you'll be up and at 'em again."

She had checked in at the Lakeshore on her way to the hockey game. Now, as they escorted her to the door, they heard a great commotion in the lobby. Al, the manager, was struggling with a couple of dishevelled citizens who were bawling insults and trying to get at each other's throats.

"We'll beat those bums of yours by five goals," howled one of the combatants.

"Outside, both of you." Al was not a large man, but he had commando training — a decided asset in the Lakeshore. "Do you want me to lose my licence?"

Slewfoot held the door open, and McGonigle and Mrs. Dinwoodie stepped nimbly aside as Al disengaged himself. The belligerents reeled into the snow.

"They've been fighting in the beer parlour all night." Al straightened his necktie. "The more beer, the more argument. The more argument, the more beer."

"Old-timers' game?" inquired Slewfoot.

"What else? Hockey causes more battles around here than religion."

"Tomorrow night," Slewfoot explained to McGonigle. "Big game of the year. There's this place Golden Valley, about thirty miles up the line. They've got a lot of old-time hockey players."

"So have we," said Al. "But they nearly always beat us."

"Three years and running. It's cost me a hatful," mourned Slewfoot.

Al said it had cost everybody a hatful, but it couldn't go on forever. A day would come. Slewfoot agreed. He had always bet a hundred on Snowshoe Lake, and he was anxious to do it again.

"But if you don't think you'll win, why do you keep on betting?" Emma wanted to know.

Slewfoot stared at her.

"Why shouldn't we? Maybe we've got a lousy old-timers' team but nobody can say we ain't good sports."

"All I can say is that you must be gluttons for punishment. Why don't you give up?"

"If we gave up," Slewfoot said indignantly, "there wouldn't *be* any Gold Cup Game. Like I said, we're good sports."

"Goodnight, good sports," said Mrs. Dinwoodie. "I'm bushed." She picked up her room key.

Sounds of battle echoed from the beer parlour.

"The natives are restless tonight." Al moved off to quell the uprising.

13

Snead Makes a Deal

When Blackjack Snead met with the executive of the Snowshoe Lake Hockey Club, summoned to emergency session in Bobo's office that night, he was delighted to find that only four members could be rounded up.

An old hand at conning small-town hockey clubs into doing what he thought best for them, Mr. Snead was all for the cosy, backroom huddle as against the free-for-all club meeting where every member has his democratic say.

"The big meeting," he always declared, "is for the birds. There's always a wise guy asking stupid questions. Give me a nice, tidy little executive meeting where we all understand each other, and I'll be home free every time."

The four members were Uncle Wilmer Kirby, Herman Schmauss, vice-president (who was under the impression that the boys were getting up a little poker game), Fergy MacAllister, treasurer of every organization in town because he managed the local bank, and Happy Thorpe, of Thorpe's Funeral Home and Furniture Store, secretary. As a club employee, Bobo presumably didn't count, although everyone knew he ran everything anyway.

"Men," said Uncle Wilmer, calling the meeting to order, "it's a little late, but we've got a guest here tonight who has to go back to the city tomorrow, and Bobo tells me he's got a proposition for us. So without beating around the bush I'm going to ask him to speak up and tell us what he has in mind. You've all heard of Mr. Snead, from the Bears — he was at the game tonight — so go ahead, Mr. Snead, we're all listening."

Mr. Snead's opening remarks were of a complimentary nature. He praised their fine little town, he praised the rink, he praised the hockey fans, he even praised the invigorating weather. It was always a pleasure, he told them, to come to Northern Ontario where the finest traditions of hockey were preserved in such towns as Snowshoe Lake.

"But I know and you know," he said, coming directly to the point, "that it costs money."

"Right," interjected Fergy MacAllister, who knew the exact amount of the overdraft at the moment.

"You gentlemen work hard to give your community the sort of hockey it deserves, and I doubt if you get very much thanks for your untiring efforts."

"You can say that again," observed Uncle Wilmer, with bitter recollections of the last annual meeting, when a card-carrying member had risen to state his considered opinion that the entire executive was a bunch of lunkheads.

"In a community of this size, if you depend on gate receipts alone, you fight a losing battle. Every year you wind up with a deficit. Every year you find it more difficult to hold your hometown players, and as for attracting good boys from outside, it's impossible. If it weren't for public-spirited citizens such as yourselves, giving freely of your time and energy, digging into your own pockets at the end of the season, backing the club's notes at the bank, hockey in Snowshoe Lake would probably fold up tomorrow."

The public-spirited citizens nodded solemnly. Blackjack Snead spoke no less than the truth. Every spring they did kick in to make up the deficit and had to wait for the first gate receipts next season before they got the money back.

"But where would the great game of hockey be without you?" asked Snead. "Where would it be without the self-sacrificing efforts of men like you in towns and villages all over Canada? And I'll ask you another question, and believe me, I know the answer as well as you do." He lowered his voice. "Where would big-league professional hockey be without you?"

"Hear! Hear!" Herman Schmauss slapped the table. "Now you're talking!"

"The answer, of course, is that without grassroots hockey we'd be dead." Blackjack Snead looked around the table. "We would wither on the vine."

He paused impressively to let the dread prospect sink in.

"It would be selfish and short-sighted of us to expect you to bear the whole burden of developing the young players on whom the future of professional hockey depends," declared Snead in ringing tones. "For that reason our organization has embarked upon a policy of expansion, with special emphasis on our farm system."

His listeners gazed at him with respect. Blackjack Snead wasn't talking like a hockey scout; he sounded more like the president of General Motors. "The whole burden...our organization has embarked...policy of expansion...special emphasis...." This was heady stuff. You had to pay attention to a man who did you the honour of using four-dollar expressions of that nature.

"We took a map of Canada, and we divided it into regions. In each of those regions we chose areas where we have not been well represented in the past. In each of those areas," he continued, now sounding like a vice-president in charge of sales management, "we pinpointed certain communities which seemed to lend themselves favourably to sponsorship. I am delighted to tell you that Snowshoe Lake is among those chosen communities, standing very high on the list, I might add."

Members of the executive exchanged gratified looks.

Here they had been under the impression that Blackjack Snead was in Snowshoe Lake bent on grabbing off their best hockey player. Instead, he came as a harbinger of good will, full of zeal for the betterment of the club.

"Frankly," said Snead, "a few of our directors thought our expansion program in Northern Ontario should be directed to one of the larger cities — Timmins, Sudbury, or Kirkland Lake. I couldn't agree. Our tentative final choice was Snowshoe Lake, and after seeing your town, meeting your manager, inspecting your arena, and watching your fine young team in action, and especially after realizing that you have a dedicated hockey public, fans who will give 100 per cent support to their club, win or lose, I am prepared to recommend that our choice be confirmed. Gentlemen, I am happy to announce that my organization will sponsor your club."

With a fine sense of timing, Mr. Snead awaited their applause. It came, as he knew it would. They were a little confused by the Snead rhetoric, but obviously he was conferring an enormous favour upon them so they applauded spontaneously. Mr. Snead responded with a modest little bow, accepting the tribute as no more than a public benefactor's due.

"We like to be generous with the clubs under our sponsorship," he resumed. "In the first place we contribute an annual sum to help cover your operating expenses. The amount, in your case, based on population, would be one thousand dollars. We would also transfer promising junior players to you, as needed, from other clubs in our junior farm system. Our objective would be a Snowshoe Lake Junior Hockey Club strong enough to contend for the Northern Ontario Hockey championship and eventually the Memorial Cup."

They goggled. They all but swooned.

"Memorial Cup!" gulped Herman Schmauss.

"That's what I said," repeated Snead, firmly.

You could mesmerize any junior hockey club executive by conjuring up a vision of the Cup. This was the moment for producing the sponsorship contract from his inside coat pocket. He placed it on the table in front of Uncle Wilmer.

"If you gentlemen will sign this on behalf of your club, I'll forward it to our headquarters office first thing in the morning and we'll be in business."

Uncle Wilmer reached for his spectacles and unfolded the contract. It was five pages long and no more involved than a federal agreement on freight rates; one qualifying clause alone wandered through a wilderness of three hundred words; and much of it was set in type so small that it baffled the naked eye. It would have taken an hour and a half to read it all the way through, and Snead knew of no one who had ever even tried. After a studious glance, Uncle Wilmer passed it along to Fergy MacAllister, acknowledged expert in legal doubletalk.

"All I want to know," said Uncle Wilmer, "is how will this affect my nephew?"

"Nephew?" Snead looked blank.

"Tim Beckett. The one who scored all them goals tonight."

"Oh yes. Very promising young forward, I recall. Well, of course, as sponsors we'll be anxious to do all we can for any of your players. Perhaps in a couple of years if he thinks he'd care to try out with one of our class A clubs we'd be glad to arrange it."

"How about his education?"

"We certainly wouldn't want him to leave school, if that's what you mean. Don't believe in it. As a matter of fact, if he made Junior A we'd encourage him to go on to college — even pay his tuition."

"One little thing," said Herman Schmauss. He glanced shrewdly at his fellow-members of the executive. "Might as well get all we can before we sign. Tomorrow night," he told Snead, "is the Old-timers' Game. We haven't won in three years. Maybe you could give us a little help."

"How?"

"Mostly we lose because our goalie is too much of an old-timer. Maybe you could find us a goalie somewhere?"

"By tomorrow night? That's a big order." Snead thought it over. Sometimes they threw the damnedest curves. "How old is an old-timer?"

"Thirty-five years old, he's got to be."

"Exhibition game?"

"It's an exhibition all right," said Happy Thorpe. "But the boys don't fool."

"How about the residence rule?"

Happy shook his head.

"There isn't any. That's what makes it interesting. Last year they rung in Bumps O'Leary on us. Used to play for Detroit. Only lasted twenty minutes, but he got three goals."

"It would be nice to get even," remarked Fergy.

"You want a good goalie, over thirty-five, in town by tomorrow night." Snead snapped his fingers. "I have him. The very man."

"Who?" asked Uncle Wilmer.

"A goalie good enough to beat any club you can dig up."

"Who?" they yelled in chorus.

Blackjack Snead smiled.

"Unbeatable Charlie Bates," he said calmly.

They couldn't have been more incredulous if the snap of his fingers had produced Unbeatable Bates in person, then and there.

"You can get Unbeatable Charlie Bates to play goal for us here tomorrow night?" exclaimed Fergy. Long years in the banking business had made him skeptical. "You must be kidding."

"I'll deliver him here tomorrow afternoon, all wrapped up and ready to go," promised Snead. "Now if you gentlemen care to sign this agreement..."

Happy Thorpe reached for a pen.

"I'm signing now before you change your mind. Man alive! I can just see that Golden Valley bunch waving their money around, begging us to take it away from them."

"You won't let us down, Mr. Snead?" said Herman Schmauss.

"My word is my bond."

"Gentlemen," said Bobo Strowger, when they had all signed, "this means a new deal in hockey for Snowshoe Lake."

"It means a new deal for the Old-timers' Game, that's for sure," chuckled Happy Thorpe. "Unbeatable Bates! Wow! We'll clobber them."

They shook hands all around. On their way out, the only member of the executive not entirely jubilant was Uncle Wilmer Kirby.

"Kinda wish that McGonigle fellow had shown up," he said. "Might have made a better deal playin' one of them against the other. Wonder whatever happened to him."

As he returned to the Lakeshore with the agreement in his pocket, Blackjack Snead was also wondering what had happened to McGonigle.

"Imagine," he mused. "All togged out like the mad trapper, pretending he's somebody else's brother. One thing about McGonigle, you can always count on him to set it up for you."

He hoped the day would never come when he no longer got a kick out of making a chump of Skates McGonigle. But it was almost too easy. McGonigle always gave him so much help.

14

The "Nomdayploom" Backfires

Anyone who locks the door of his house in Snowshoe Lake leaves himself wide open to public reproach as an inhospitable character, lacking in social virtue.

Besides, it's a nuisance. Friends and neighbours who drop in during one's absence have to kick in the back door or pry open a window. It is rude to subject anyone to all this trouble.

Slewfoot Shannon was not surprised, therefore, when he saw lamplight shining through the window as he approached his cabin that night with Skates McGonigle.

"Looks like we got company." Pleased, he opened the door.

Slewfoot had company indeed. Wedged in the wicker chair, where he had been studying one of Slewfoot's collection of comic books while he waited, was a stout man in a blue uniform with brass buttons.

"Goshamighty, we've been raided. Whatcha doing here, Chief?"

Telesphore Renaud, who constituted the entire police force of Snowshoe Lake, set aside the comic book.

"Who is your friend, Slewfoot?"

"Friend? This here is no friend. He's my brother. You've heard me talk about my brother Abner?"

"No," said the chief.

"Well, this is him, anyway. Ab, shake hands with the chief."

As the chief heaved himself out of the chair McGonigle decided it was high time he put an end to the masquerade. There was no further point to it. Mrs. Beckett was already aware of his identity and besides he had made up his mind to do a little missionary work with the hockey club first thing in the morning.

"Look, Slewfoot," he said. "I think maybe we'd better explain..."

"One moment," interrupted Renaud. He held up a big hand and made a beckoning motion with an imperative finger. "The identification."

"What do you mean?" demanded Slewfoot. "I've already told you. He's my brother."

Renaud ignored him. The finger beckoned again.

"You have papers?" he asked McGonigle. "The identification that you are Abner Shannon?"

"Now just a darn minute," yelped Slewfoot. "What's this all about? You mean you doubt my word?"

"Identification," insisted Renaud.

"Sure I have identification. But what I'm trying to tell you..."

"Don't tell him a thing," clamoured Slewfoot, wedging himself between McGonigle and the chief. "What's the big idea coming in here and annoying my brother?"

"Lay off, Slewfoot," McGonigle said. "You're not helping me a bit."

"Your wallet, please. The identification that you are Abner Shannon."

"You got a warrant?" shouted Slewfoot. "Can't search anyone without a warrant."

McGonigle produced his wallet.

"But I'm not Abner Shannon. That's what I'm trying to tell you."

"Aha!" said the chief. "You admit it."

"Admit nothing," howled Slewfoot. "Make him show a warrant. You watch out what you're doing, Chief, or you're going to be sorry."

The chief took the wallet.

"One more word out of you, Slewfoot," he said wearily, "and I run you in for making moonshine whiskey."

"You snoop! You've been looking under my bunk."

The chief sniffed.

"No need to look. I have a nose." He opened the wallet. "Now then, let us have a look at this identification."

"It's all there, but not for anyone called Shannon. My name is McGonigle. Most people call me Skates. I'm a hockey scout."

The chief examined the contents of the wallet. He shook his head.

"Uh-uh," he said.

"What do you mean, uh-uh?"

"I mean uh-uh your name is not McGonigle."

"Look at my Blueshirt card. Can't you read?"

"I can read, yes. In both English *and* French. But this is not your identification because this is not your wallet."

"What gives you that idea?"

"Because I spoke with Mr. Skates McGonigle on the telephone not more than one hour ago. You are not Mr. McGonigle any more than you are Slewfoot's brother. I think you had better come along with me."

Slewfoot hopped around like a man with a tack in his foot.

"Chief, you're out of your mind. You can't pinch this guy. How could you talk to him on the phone when he hasn't been out of my sight since he hit town?"

"Slewfoot, first you tell me he is your brother. Now he tells me he is somebody else. How long have you known this man?"

"Since five o'clock this afternoon. Emma Dinwoodie brought him here so he could hide out for a while."

"Hide out?" The chief frowned. "That is all I need to know. Innocent men do not hide."

"If you'll just listen to me for a minute," said McGonigle, "I can explain."

"Explain to me first how you come to have Mr. McGonigle's wallet in your pocket."

"That's easy. Because I *am* Mr. McGonigle, and it's my wallet."

"It is not easy. Because Mr. McGonigle phoned to warn me about an imposter using his credit cards and wallet."

"Some nut is accusing me of stealing my own wallet?"

"Not a nut, Mr. McGonigle. And if you ask why he phoned me it is because the wallet contained return plane and bus tickets to Snowshoe Lake where he had planned to attend the hockey game tonight. He will be pleased to hear that his wallet has been recovered. Let us go."

"Go where?"

"The police station, naturally. That is where we lock up strangers who have wallets which do not belong to them and pretend to be somebody else."

In his constabulary career Chief Telesphore Renaud had learned that few people take kindly to arrest, and that his customers, as he called them, invariably insisted that it was all a big mistake. In this case matters ran true to form; the outraged protests were merely noisier than usual. Even when they arrived at the modest building which served Snowshoe Lake as police headquarters and lock-up (with a dog pound at the back) the uproar had not diminished.

McGonigle, beginning to suspect that Blackjack Snead lurked somewhere behind his plight, although he hadn't figured out how, bellowed that he was the victim of a despicable plot and demanded a lawyer. The chief said the only lawyer in town was presently out of town, attending Assizes in Haileybury. Slewfoot kept chanting, "Yon's an innocent man," until the chief threatened to lock him up too, for disturbing the peace.

Methodically, the chief went about the formalities of booking McGonigle in for the night. Telesphore Renaud was not easily moved by eloquent appeals to his better nature; fervent denials of guilt impressed him not at all. When Telesphore Renaud had the goods on a customer there was merely one simple rule — pop him in the pokey, and let him tell it to the court.

Booking the prisoner presented one awkward little problem. He declined to give his real name, kept insisting that it was McGonigle, which the chief refused to accept on the sensible ground that it would contradict the charge and amount to a written confession of departmental error.

"You are accused of stealing Mr. McGonigle's wallet," he explained patiently. "Therefore you cannot be Mr. McGonigle."

He was annoyed when McGonigle couldn't see the logic of this. The problem was solved by registering the culprit as John Doe, alias McGonigle, alias Shannon, with a large question mark after each name. The chief then produced a cotton sack in which he placed the wallet, along with McGonigle's watch, keys, and small change, listed these items, gave McGonigle a receipt and deposited the sack, duly tagged, in the office safe. He removed a bunch of keys from a nail and unlocked the door leading to the cells in the back room.

"Man, oh man!" said McGonigle, heavily. "Are you going to be sorry! False arrest. I'll sue you for a million dollars."

Telesphore Renaud was unperturbed. He had heard it all before. The amount was always an even million — never more, never a cent less. And none of them ever sued.

At this stage Slewfoot abandoned the policy of making a nuisance of himself. Clearly, nothing was to be gained by it.

"I'm going to fetch Emma," he told McGonigle, and headed for the door. "Don't go away."

The cell door clanged, McGonigle sat down on the cot.

"I'll be out of here in five minutes," he told the chief. "Mrs. Dinwoodie will identify me."

"You have known Mrs. Dinwoodie for a long time?"

McGonigle thought that one over.

"Long enough."

Telesphore Renaud was not impressed. Mrs. Dinwoodie's identification, if she offered any at all, would be on the same order as Slewfoot's.

"Good night."

"Hey, wait a minute. Where are you going?"

"Home. It is very late. My wife worries."

"But Mrs. Dinwoodie will be here in a few minutes. She won't let me down."

"I am very tired," said the chief, "and tomorrow will be a heavy day. The Old-timers' Game. Always it makes fights." He looked at his watch. "Very well. Ten minutes."

He went out into the office and picked up the phone. It would be too late to call Mr. Skates McGonigle back long-distance (he had, in any case, forgotten to leave his home number), but a telegram would reach his office early in the morning. The chief dialed the railway telegraph office. He dictated a message, collect, informing McGonigle of the recovery of his wallet.

"Am holding suspect who claims to be you," he said, and concluded by notifying McGonigle that he would be expected to come to Snowshoe Lake to identify the wallet and appear as a Crown witness in magistrate's court. That done, he put his feet up on the desk and waited for Mrs. Dinwoodie. A fine woman, of excellent reputation. She would be embarrassed to learn how she had been taken in by this imposter. Perhaps she had even loaned the fellow money, in which case there could be further charges. Telesphore Renaud picked up his copy of the Criminal Code and thumbed through it in search of the sections dealing with impersonation and false pretenses.

Emma Dinwoodie was putting her hair up in curlers, and Blackjack Snead was examining junior players' certificates in his adjacent room at the Lakeshore when Slewfoot Shannon thundered up the stairs.

"Emma!" he panted. "You awake?"

"Who's that?"

"It's me. Slewfoot."

"Go away, Slewfoot."

"I've got to talk to you. About Skates. He's in terrible trouble."

The Lakeshore was not of sturdy construction. A heavy snorer on the first floor had been known to disturb the slumbers of guests on the third. Slewfoot's arrival became something of a public event, arousing special interest in Room 12.

"What kind of trouble?"

"Big trouble. He's in jail."

"Come off it, Slewfoot. A joke's a joke but I'm tired. Go away."

"No foolin'. He's in the cooler right this minute. We've got to get him out."

Emma sighed and proceeded to open the door. This operation took a little tine. From past experience she had learned that in the Lakeshore mere possession of a room key was no guarantee against invasion by wandering guests, usually befuddled. First, she removed a chair which she had prudently jammed beneath the doorknob. Then she tugged at a bolt which she had pounded into place with a Gideon Bible. Not that she had been assailed by fears for her chastity. These were merely the normal precautions taken by any sensible guest to discourage visitors who might interrupt a good night's rest. Now she turned the key and yanked vigorously at the door, which stuck. She braced herself with one foot against the frame and hauled away, while Slewfoot applied a helpful shoulder against the other side. The door flew open. Slewfoot shot into the room.

"Now then," she said severely and hitched her dressing gown around her, "so help me, Slewfoot, if you two are pulling some stupid joke I'll clobber the pair of you."

"It's no joke. You've got to come down to the jail. The poor guy is locked in a cell. With iron bars on it."

"In heaven's name, what for?"

"Nothing. He didn't do a thing. An innocent man. I told the chief a dozen times. 'Yon's an innocent man,' I said. But he wouldn't listen."

"Now listen, Slewfoot. It isn't half an hour since you two left me. How could McGonigle get into trouble in that time? What did he do?"

"Believe it or not, Emma, he's in jail for stealing his own wallet."

"You're not making sense."

"And for pretending to be himself. Ever hear the like of that?"

"I do wish you would calm down and talk like a rational human being."

"It's on account of him not being my brother. Now the chief won't believe he's anybody."

"What started all this?"

"The chief says he got a phone call. Long-distance. From Skates McGonigle himself."

"Impossible."

"Chief says McGonigle told him this guy pinched his wallet and is going around the country pretending to be *him*."

"Rubbish." She pushed Slewfoot out of the room. "Wait downstairs. I'll be with you in a minute."

In the hall, Slewfoot hesitated, scratching his head.

"Emma?"

"Downstairs."

"I'm beginning to wonder."

"Beat it. I want to get dressed."

"Maybe we've been taken. Maybe the guy isn't McGonigle after all."

"Slewfoot, you're an idiot."

The door slammed. Slewfoot trudged off downstairs.

"Come to think of it," he muttered, "I never did see the fellow in my whole life until this afternoon. Could be he's a real scamp."

15

Maybelle's Buttons

Emma Dinwoodie didn't even take time to remove the aluminumware from her head. She was dressed and out of her room in five minutes. When the door slammed behind her and she went hurrying downstairs her neighbour in Room 12 chuckled happily.

This would even up for the time McGonigle had conned him into going all the way to Port Arthur to scout a super-duper goalie on a club called the Lakehead Wildcats. Red McCloskey was the goalie's name. Seven consecutive shutouts. The record was impressive. But the club turned out to be a girl's hockey club. It had taken Snead months to live it down.

In a few minutes now he would be summoned to the jail, McGonigle begging him to come over and supply identification. They would be telling the story in every dressing room in the country for the next ten years.

Over at the police station Emma stormed in like a metallic-topped angel of fury, with Slewfoot at her heels.

"What's going on here?" she demanded. "I understand you've got a very good friend of mine locked up on some silly excuse. Let him out at once."

Telesphore Renaud sighed. These women! They always began by ordering him about and when that didn't work they cajoled, pleaded, begged, and finally fell back on the ultimate weapon of tears. It was his great virtue as an officer of the law that once he determined the course of duty he was not to be moved from it. With dignity, he heaved himself out of his chair and led the way to the cells, where McGonigle sat moodily on his cot.

"A flaming disgrace!" snapped Emma. "One of the greatest men in Canada caged up like a common pickpocket! All right, what are you waiting for? Turn him loose."

"You identify this man?"

"Of course. Skates McGonigle, the hockey player. Mean to say you don't recognize him? Where have you been all your life?"

It was another of Telesphore Renaud's virtues in an unenviable job that he never lost his temper, although it was often sorely tried.

"How long have you known him?" he said, patiently.

"I've known *of* him for years. Everybody knows Skates McGonigle. Flew up with him this afternoon. Come on, Renaud, use your head."

"I am using it. When did you first meet this man?"

"At the airport, this afternoon."

"And you have merely his word for it that he is Mr. McGonigle." The chief shook his head. "It is not sufficient. You have been deceived, Mrs. Dinwoodie. This man took advantage of your kindness."

"Nobody takes advantage of Emma Dinwoodie."

"I need a good lawyer," said McGonigle.

"You don't need anyone except somebody who's known you more than twenty-four hours. Think hard, Skates. Isn't there anyone in town besides us? How about Bobo Strowger?"

"Never met the guy in my life."

"*I* know!" shouted Slewfoot. "Why didn't I think of it before? Blackjack Snead!"

"The very man," said Emma.

McGonigle leaped from the cot. "No!" he howled. "Never!"

"But he can identify you. Hasn't he known you for years?"

"I don't want him to even hear about this. He's the last man in Canada I want to see around this jail, unless he's in the next cell. Think I want him coming in here gloating over me? Do you know what Snead would do?"

"Laugh?" said Slewfoot.

"Oh, he'll do that, all right. He'll be laughing for the next twenty-five years, if he lives that long, all over the country. But if you send for him he's just as liable to look me over and hide a big grin and say, 'Sorry, folks, I never saw this guy in my life.'"

"He wouldn't," Emma said.

"Wouldn't he? You don't know Blackjack Snead. That's exactly what he would do, because that's the kind of joker he is. And he'd think it was real funny. Oh no! Of all people, don't tell Snead."

"I can see your point," she agreed. "But you can't stay here, that's for sure." She opened her purse and turned to the chief. "How much will it take to bail him out?"

"I cannot grant bail. Only a justice of the peace can do that."

"Okay. Where can I find a justice of the peace?"

"At this hour?"

"If you can toss a man into the pokey at this hour, I can wake up a JP"

"There is Wilmer Kirby," the chief said reluctantly, "but he will not like it."

Mr. Kirby did not like it. Routed out of bed in his living quarters over the store, he growled and grumbled like a sea lion. But when Emma Dinwoodie explained the purpose of her rescue mission his irritation faded.

"Been wondering what happened to that fellow," he said. "Wait till I get my pants on."

By the time he rejoined Mrs. Dinwoodie and Slewfoot he had come to a decision. As a leading citizen of Snowshoe Lake, it occurred to him that the good name of his community was in peril. He could see the headlines in the *Northern News*, the *Timmins Advance*, the *North Bay Nugget*, the *New Liskeard Speaker*: "Famous Visitor Jailed by Mistake."

He could hear the newscasters: "Faces were red and the air was blue in Snowshoe Lake last night when one of hockeydom's all-time greats landed in the hoosegow. Skates McGonigle, who arrived in Snowshoe Lake on a goodwill tour and got the bum's rush instead of a royal welcome, is today threatening to sue the town for half a million dollars…"

Uncle Wilmer broke into a sweat.

"Bail isn't enough," he announced. "I can fix that in two minutes. But we've got to get him out for good and hush the whole thing up."

He reached for the phone. When a sleepy voice answered he said, "Tim. Your Uncle Wilmer. Those hockey pictures you've got all over your wall. Have you one of Skates McGonigle?"

"Sure thing. Why?"

"I need it right away. I'll be there in five minutes."

They piled into Uncle Wilmer's car and zoomed three blocks. Tim, fully dressed by now and wide-eyed with curiosity, produced a page which had been clipped from a sports magazine, with a picture of McGonigle.

"What's it all about?" Tim wanted to know. "Mom said he was here tonight. Boy, was I ever sorry I missed him. What's happened? Why do you need the picture?"

McGonigle, massive of shoulders and bulging out of a Blueshirt uniform, was depicted in heroic pose, gripping a stick and glowering belligerently at some invisible opponent. Mrs. Dinwoodie and Slewfoot studied the picture in dismay.

"Doesn't look much like him," muttered Slewfoot.

"They got him all prettied up," Mrs. Dinwoodie said.

"Must have been taken a long time ago. When he had hair."

Mrs. Beckett, in her dressing gown, said, "Is that the same fellow who was here tonight? My goodness, he took on some weight since then. Hardly know it was the same person."

"It was when he broke into the NHL," Tim explained. "I guess he's changed some."

"Forty pounds more of him if there's an ounce," declared Emma Dinwoodie.

"Only picture you've got?" Uncle Wilmer rubbed his chin doubtfully. "We need it to get him out of jail."

"Jail!" exploded Tim. "Skates McGonigle in *jail*? What did he do?"

"He come here under a nomdayploom," said Slewfoot.

"And it backfired on him." Emma folded up the picture. "It'll have to do. But I don't think the chief's going to buy it."

"I can get another picture." Tim grabbed his jacket and headed for the door. "Won't take a minute."

"Where you going, son?" asked Mrs. Beckett.

"Maybelle. She has tons of them."

Maybelle Peever, that devout fan, was a collector of hockey buttons. A button, which buttoned nothing and had no practical purpose of any kind, but which came in a packet of gum and was imprinted with a portrait of a hockey player — this was what Maybelle treasured, traded, and accumulated. Her private collection of hockey buttons was acknowledged by the small fry of Snowshoe Lake to be unequalled in rarity and scope.

Tim Beckett's request for the loan of a McGonigle button at twelve-thirty of a cold winter night set off an epic commotion in the Peever household.

Not that Maybelle objected to being awakened. Not that she was averse to putting the collection on view. She merely insisted on lugging it to the police station in person. Her parents protested. Her brothers and sisters crowded into the living room in their nightshirts, all yelling at once. Maybelle out-shrieked everyone. If one of her hockey buttons could be the magic token that would open jail doors for a victim of injustice — said victim being a legendary hockey hero — she had a right to be there.

"And if I can't go, I won't lend you my McGonigle button," she said, clutching a paper sack. "It's in this bag and I'm the only one who can find it."

"Stubborn as a mule!" gritted Maybelle's exasperated mother. "We might as well let her go, Pa, or she'll howl for the rest of the night. Get dressed, you obstinate child."

She still clung to the sack when they drove to the police station. Before they left, Tim and Uncle Wilmer tried to persuade her to let them inspect the McGonigle button, but Maybelle asked scornfully if they thought she was stupid.

"You'd take the button and leave me at home."

Telesphore Renaud was snoozing in his chair with his feet on the desk when the rescue party arrived, led by a tow-headed child who promptly dumped the entire contents of a paper sack on to his desk.

"He's in there," Maybelle announced.

Chief Renaud blinked at a vast mound of plastic buttons. Some of them spilled off the desk and went skipping and rolling to various corners of the office.

"Chief," boomed Uncle Wilmer, "I want that fellow set loose. Not just on bail. I want him loose. Because you've got the wrong man."

"And here's a picture to prove it." Tim produced his evidence. Telesphore Renaud inspected the picture with neither enthusiasm nor recognition. "Skates McGonigle, when he used to play hockey," Tim insisted. Renaud shook his head. He opened the door to the cell room.

"Go back and look. They are not the same."

"Good grief, you're a hard man to convince," Emma Dinwoodie exploded.

"He's here somewhere." Maybelle pawed the hillock of buttons.

"What is all this rubbish?" inquired the chief.

"It isn't rubbish. It's hockey buttons. Pictures of all the great players. I've been saving them for ages. They come with gum."

"Lordy, child! You must like gum," marvelled Mrs. Dinwoodie.

"I don't. I hate it. But I like hockey buttons. Here's a Dit Clapper, and a Turk Broda —"

Telesphore Renaud spied a familiar, legendary face. He snapped it up.

"Ha!"

"That him?" asked Slewfoot.

"Maurice Richard!" exclaimed the chief. "The greatest. What a player!"

"I'd give you an argument on that," said Uncle Wilmer. "You ever see Howie Morenz? Or Apps? Stewart never saw the day."

"Maurice Richard," shouted the chief, "was the greatest hockey player who ever lived. There will be nobody else like him, ever."

"I guess you never saw Morenz," said Uncle Wilmer, getting red in the face. "You wouldn't talk like that if you did. Just because Morenz wasn't a Frenchman you fellows never could see him."

"Let us leave race prejudice out of this," said Telesphore Renaud, darkly. "How many goals did Morenz ever score? More than Richard? Ha!"

"The schedules were shorter in his day," bellowed Uncle Wilmer. "I admit Richard scored a lot of goals. I'm not taking anything away from Richard. But you can't compare him with Morenz."

"I *know* I've got a Skates McGonigle," yelped Maybelle. "I had to trade a Busher Jackson and an Eddie Shore for him. He's awfully scarce."

"Morenz!" Telesphore Renaud glared at Uncle Wilmer. "The Canadiens traded him."

"Stupidest thing the Frenchmen ever did was let Morenz go. And don't forget they brought him back and glad to have him. Look, Renaud, don't start comparin' hockey players, until you've seen 'em all."

"Did you ever see this McGonigle?"

"No, I've got to admit I didn't, or I'd have him outta that cell so fast it'd make your head swim. He's comin' out anyway, because I'm gonna grant bail..."

"Here he is!" shrieked Maybelle. "I found him." She held up a button. The chief studied it. He frowned. Then he opened the door to the cell room, with Maybelle at his heels. The others followed. Behind the bars, McGonigle looked up gloomily from his cot.

"Why of course it's Skates McGonigle!" Maybelle screeched. "It couldn't be anyone else." She stared reproachfully at Telesphore Renaud. "You shouldn't keep a great hockey player like him in jail. It just isn't right."

With great deliberation Telesphore Renaud gazed at McGonigle, then at the button, then at McGonigle again. It was fortunate for McGonigle that the button photograph had been taken late in his career.

"Oh come off it, Chief," said Uncle Wilmer, over his shoulder. "Give or take a few pounds, it's a spittin' image."

"When Mr. McGonigle called up on the long distance, he warned me there would be a resemblance," the chief muttered.

"Nobody called you on the long distance," bellowed McGonigle. "And if somebody did it certainly wasn't me. More likely a low down, conniving smart aleck called Blackjack Snead."

"Let him out, Chief," said Uncle Wilmer. "If you're not convinced I'll order bail."

Telesphore Renaud unlocked the cell door. Rumpled, McGonigle emerged. He nodded at Tim.

"Hi, lad," he said. "I saw you play tonight. You did all right."

"My name is Kirby," said Uncle Wilmer, extending his hand. "On behalf of the town of Snowshoe Lake I want to apologize for the mistake what's been made here."

"I am not so sure it has been a mistake," insisted Telesphore Renaud.

"You can thank this little girl here for getting you out," Uncle Wilmer continued. "She collects buttons."

"It's an honour to meet you, Mr. McGonigle." Maybelle had her book in readiness. "Could I have your autograph, please sir?"

McGonigle signed.

"A fine thing," snapped Emma. "Mr. McGonigle comes all the way up here to look at a hockey player and he gets treated like a pickpocket. I hope he sues."

"Thank you, little girl." McGonigle returned the book. "No hard feelings," he told Uncle Wilmer. He shook hands with Tim. "I want to get together with you tomorrow morning for a little talk."

"Won't do you no good," Uncle Wilmer said, sadly.

"What do you mean, Uncle Wilmer?" asked Tim.

"Too bad we didn't know Mr. McGonigle was in town. We already signed."

"Signed what?"

"We've already signed up with Mr. Snead's outfit to sponsor the hockey club," said Uncle Wilmer in a dismal voice.

Emma glared at him.

"You *signed*?"

Uncle Wilmer nodded.

"If we'd known Mr. McGonigle was here..."

"Your club gave Snead sponsorship?" said McGonigle. "Don't you know what it means?"

"It's going to help us. We get out of debt. They'll send us some players."

"But Snead can take this boy away from you. And he will. He's done it with other clubs."

"Can't take me if I don't want to go," said Tim.

"That's what you think." McGonigle turned to Uncle Wilmer. "When did you do this?"

"Tonight. Executive meeting after the game."

"Your friend Snead doesn't waste any time," observed Mrs. Dinwoodie.

Telesphore Renaud had been very thoughtful. "Mr. McGonigle," he said, "did you ever see Howie Morenz play?"

"When I was a kid. Why?"

"Was he better than Maurice Richard?"

McGonigle considered.

"I wouldn't say that. They were different."

Telesphore Renaud looked at Uncle Wilmer.

"See!" he said.

16

No Help from Dooley

When Unbeatable Bates bowed out of major league hockey at the age of thirty-five, everybody said it was a great shame and a loss to the sport, and his employers made public pronouncements to the effect that there would always be a place in the organization for the Unbeatable. Privately they said it was too bad he had become a little twitchy, but if a goalie insists on stopping pucks with his ears what else can you expect?

So the Unbeatable bade farewell to the big-time arenas and floated around the fringe as sometime manager, occasional coach, and itinerant goalkeeper, available for odd jobs anywhere, any time. An 8 a.m. phone call from Blackjack Snead, somewhere out on the frostbite-and-chilblain circuit, was nothing new to Unbeatable Bates.

"Away up *there*?" exclaimed the Unbeatable, as if Snead had proposed an expedition to the Bering Sea. "How many days does it take to get to the place, and where do I hire a dog team?"

"The game is tonight," said Blackjack Snead, "and you fly."

"Two hundred bucks?" suggested the Unbeatable, hopefully.

"One hundred and expenses."

"Slave labour."

"The bus from the airport gets here at five o'clock. Be on it!" ordered Blackjack Snead. He hung up and proceeded to other calls. Some of them involved sports writers and commentators.

"When a deal seems a little shaky," Blackjack Snead always said, "get it into the newspapers as soon as you can. Somehow it always looks twice as true when you see it in print."

Other phones were busy that morning. With Emma Dinwoodie and Mrs. Beckett breathing down the back of his neck, Uncle Wilmer Kirby called an emergency meeting of the hockey club. Not just the executive — the whole club.

"I was afraid of that," groaned Bobo when he heard the news.

"I wasn't," said Snead. "But I expected it."

"McGonigle is out of jail. He'll try to bust the agreement."

"Ho-ho-ho."

"Just the same, you'd better be at that meeting."

"Why?"

"To defend the agreement."

"It doesn't need defending. It's already signed. But I'll do even better. I'll explain it."

The meeting was called for noon in the Legion Hall. All the members didn't show up, nor were they expected; some were toiling on day shift in the depths of Snowshoe Mine; but Wednesday half holiday and the mood of celebration induced by the Old-timers' Game made for what Uncle Wilmer called "a mighty good turnout." There was a great buzz of interest when Skates McGonigle arrived in the company of Slewfoot.

Mr. McGonigle looked a little subdued, but he submitted to a lot of handshaking; and practically everyone in the hall was crowding around for the privilege, when an outburst of cheering heralded the arrival of Blackjack Snead, escorted by an apprehensive Bobo Strowger.

"Skates, old man!" Blackjack Snead was exuberantly cordial. The handshake was firm. The slap on the shoulder was that of an old pal. "I heard you were in town. Wonderful to see you again."

"Think so?" grunted McGonigle.

"I heard you had a little trouble with the police," exclaimed Snead, in ringing tones that could be heard throughout the hall. "Why didn't you give me a call?"

"Nothing serious," replied McGonigle. "Somebody heard I was a hockey scout, so right away the cops figured I must be a suspicious character. Too many guys giving our racket a bad name."

Up on the platform, flanked by Fergy MacAllister and Happy Thorpe, Uncle Wilmer pounded the table.

"Shut up, everybody," he bawled. "This is an emergency meeting of the hockey club."

"What's the emergency, Wilmer?" piped a voice from the crowd. "Are we overdrawn at the bank again?"

This brought hearty laughter from everyone except Fergy MacAllister, who looked pained. The bank manager could never understand why an overdraft should be regarded as a subject of mirth.

Uncle Wilmer flourished a copy of the sponsorship agreement.

"This here is the emergency," he said. "This is a paper your executive signed last night for the good of the club, only now it's up to the members to say whether you want to go along with it."

"Why did you sign it, if you didn't know if we'd go along with it?" inquired a member. "What's the deal?"

"What happened is this," said Uncle Wilmer. "Mr. Snead, whom you have all heard of, came up here last night to see the game and he liked the look of our club so much he'd like us to be a farm club for the Bears."

The cheer that greeted this announcement rattled the windows. To a community which could boast no closer contact with the heroes of big-league hockey than the fact that Happy Thorpe's wife had a cousin who was once a stick boy for the old New York Americans, this was exciting news. Snowshoe Lake a professional farm club! Incredible!

"Whaddaya mean we mightn't go along with it?" roared a miner. "When do they start?"

Bobo Strowger popped to his feet.

"It starts right now, boys, this very minute. All you've got to do is ratify the agreement, which is certainly the best deal we'll ever get for hockey in this town. All you've got to do to ratify the agreement is holler yes..."

"Yes!" responded the membership in a thunderous roar.

Uncle Wilmer pounded the table.

"Will you guys kindly wait a goldarn minute?" he said. "And Bobo, will you kindly shut up until I get though talking. The point is this. Not only have we got this deal with Mr. Snead which maybe we should have waited before we signed, but what has happened is that Mr McGonigle of the Blueshirts also wants us to be a farm club for his outfit and now we've got *two* propositions."

Another joyful roar.

"What's McGonigle's proposition?" someone wanted to know. The question was echoed throughout the hall. McGonigle was hoisted to his feet.

"All I've got to say," declared McGonigle, "is that we'll give you the same terms and better." He held up a hand to curb a rising cheer. "And one thing more. We guarantee we won't take any player away from here unless he says he wants to go."

"What's the meaning of that?" demanded Bobo.

"Read your sponsorship agreement. Look at the fine print."

Uncle Wilmer was ready. He flipped the pages of the agreement.

"I guess maybe this is what Mr. McGonigle means." He studied the offending clause through his spectacles and read slowly: "'The sponsoring club reserves the right to transfer any player to any other club within its jurisdiction at any time.'" He waited a moment to let it sink in. "The way I figure it," he said, squinting over his spectacles, "is that it means the Bears could lift Tim Beckett off our hockey club next week and ship him off to some other outfit, and there isn't a thing we could do about it. I wish I'd read this thing all the way through before I stuck my John Henry on it."

Cries of "They wouldn't dare," "Let 'em try it," and "What kind of a deal is that?" They subsided when Blackjack Snead unfolded his lanky frame and rose with upraised palms as if about to pronounce a benediction.

"Gentlemen!"

Snead had put the quietus on many a belligerent meeting. He had the voice of a sergeant-major when he cared to exercise it. Perhaps it was his presence, perhaps it was his voice, perhaps it was the shock of being addressed as gentlemen, but the members of the hockey club were hushed in an instant.

"I came here," said Blackjack Snead, impressively, "to help you."

He folded his arms and turned slowly, scanning the crowd. If anyone thought of getting a laugh by remarking, "You mean you came to help yourself," he abandoned the notion.

"But now," resumed Snead, "I find my friendly intentions have been misunderstood."

He reached into his pocket and produced a document. He unfolded its pages. He held it aloft for all to see.

"This," he said, "is a sponsorship agreement. A standard document. It is designed to protect clubs and players alike. But first let me explain."

Mr. Snead's dissertation on professional hockey's recruiting methods was a bewildering masterpiece of doubletalk. His explanation of the draft was not quite as confusing as his detailed exposition of the legal niceties of the C-form but these were models of lucidity compared with his interpretation of territorial rights and player transfers.

Perhaps there is no human being alive who actually does understand the manifold rules which govern players who make their living out of hockey. These regulations are designed expressly to protect young men from being spoiled by the sort of extravagant salaries which have ruined so many promising athletes in football and baseball; it follows that they must be a little involved. So perhaps it was not entirely Snead's fault that his audience was glassy-eyed after three minutes and stupefied by the time he sat down.

What counted was the general impression. And the general impression was this: that the NHL was a benevolent organization devoted to developing sound minds in the sound bodies of Canadian youth; that Mr. Snead's club was a sort of charitable foundation which had got mixed up in pro hockey as a sideline to its real interest, the promotion of simon-pure amateur hockey in deserving communities such as Snowshoe Lake; and that Mr. Snead himself had long been a missionary in the cause, suffering privation and hunger without complaint while bringing the Word into the wilderness.

Uncle Wilmer scratched his head. He was as confused as everyone else, but he had to admit that even if he lost track of the Snead message along about the two-minute mark it certainly sounded noble. Mr. Snead's speech aroused loud, if mystified, applause and there was a great babble of conversation from which the phrase "Yes, but what the hell did he *say*?" emerged clearly. Uncle Wilmer rapped on the table.

"Thank you, Mr. Snead," he said, and was just about to ask McGonigle to state his case when Bobo Strowger popped up again.

"Well, fellows," declaimed Bobo, "there's your answer. You heard Mr. Snead. I've been managing this club a long time. For peanuts. I don't get much out of it except the satisfaction of doing something for Snowshoe Lake. Do you think I'd recommend this agreement if it wasn't for the good of the club?"

"*What* club?" inquired a heckler. "The Bears?"

"Now I call that a pretty lousy remark," said Bobo, aggrieved. "Uncalled for. You all heard Mr. Snead. He gave me his solemn promise that he won't move Tim Beckett out of here until the lad is good and ready. Can't ask anything fairer than that, can you?"

Uncle Wilmer looked hopefully at McGonigle.

"You got anything to say to that, Mr. McGonigle?"

McGonigle got to his feet.

"Maybe Mr. Snead gave your manager a solemn promise, but you won't find it anywhere in that agreement. He gave the Algonquin Falls club a solemn promise when he sponsored them. Three weeks after they signed he talked their two best forwards into turning pro. They wound up in Tulsa, Oklahoma. The Bears have pulled this on three amateur clubs this year, and I'm warning you they'll do the same to you. The minute that sponsorship deal goes through you don't control your players any more. They belong to the Bears."

"That's tellin' them!" howled Slewfoot. He leaped onto a chair. "You fellows going to stand for a deal like that? Slavery, that's what it is! It ain't democratic."

This sparked a great hubbub. Everyone had an opinion and decided to state it forthwith. Arguments broke out all over the place. Uncle Wilmer pounded the table in vain appeals for silence. Bobo Strowger leaped onto the platform.

"I'm not going to stand by and hear my friend Blackjack Snead insulted," he bawled. "Why this fellow who's got the gall to stand up here and say Mr. Snead won't live up to his promises — what do we know about him? Why we're not even sure he's got the right to speak for the Blueshirts! He spent last night in jail, charged with stealing somebody's wallet. He wants us to tear up a signed agreement, signed by our own executive — and for what? He can do better, he says. Okay, McGonigle, put up or shut up. What have you got to offer? And if you have something to offer, how do we know you can back it up? I challenge you to phone your head office right now and come up with something better." He pointed to the pay phone at the rear of the hall. "You want to take me up on that? Or are you going to back down?"

"I back down for nobody!" said McGonigle, and headed for the phone. There was a concerted rush on the part of eager members to escort him. Half a dozen of them wanted to lend him a dime.

A hush fell as McGonigle made his collect call to the Blueshirt headquarters. He heard Ginger's clear voice as she accepted the charge. He heard her say, "It's for you, Mr. Dooley. From Skates McGonigle."

"McGonigle?" yelled Dooley across leagues of snow. "Gimme that phone."

"Hello, Ben," McGonigle said, cheerfully. "Look, I've got a little problem."

"A *little* problem?" screamed Dooley. "You've got a great big problem, buster, and it's a lucky thing for you that you're three hundred miles out of my reach because otherwise I'd wring your fat neck."

The listeners crowding around the phone looked at one

another in mild astonishment. McGonigle took the receiver from his ear and inspected it for mechanical defects.

"Must have the wrong number," he muttered. He spoke into the phone. "Ben?"

"You have a lot of nerve to call me after what I just heard on the radio," Dooley bellowed. "Sammy Goldfarb on his noon sportscast says Blackjack Snead took over that club I sent you to scout."

"How did Sammy find out about that?"

"Then it's true?"

"Ben, that's why I called you."

"You gummed it up, McGonigle, and what's more I know why. Are you still in jail?"

"Jail, Ben?"

"You heard me."

"How did you find out about that, Ben?"

"From a telegram that came to this office this morning. For you. Telling you the cops picked up a guy in Snowshoe Lake claiming to be you and carrying your wallet. What kind of nonsense is that?"

"It was a case of mistaken identity, Ben."

"Listen. Did that club sign a sponsor deal with Snead?"

"Well yes, Ben, but if…"

"Including Beckett?"

"Well, yes. That's just the point, Ben. If we…"

"And you did get yourself tossed into the jug?"

"Only for a little while, Ben. It was a mistake."

"It was a mistake that I ever sent you up there in the first place, you numbskull. Nobody but a lunkhead like you could be thrown into jail for claiming to be himself. And nobody but you could be sent out to scout one hockey player and wind up losing a whole club."

The fascinated audience crowding around the phone had no trouble hearing Ben Dooley's side of the conversation. He came through loud and clear. And no one within a distance of twenty feet could have missed his next utterance.

"I mighta known you'd gum it up! McGonigle, you're fired!"

"What was that, Ben?"

"I said you're fired!" yelled Dooley. "F-i-r-e-d — fired!"

"Did you say fired, Ben?"

"Don't tell me you're deaf as well as dumb. *Yes!* Fired, bounced, finished, don't come back."

"But you can't mean that, Ben. Listen…"

Click!

"I'm at a hockey club meeting and I can iron it all out… Ben?…Ben?"

There was a time when only a figure in a fairy tale could disappear in the twinkling of an eye. But yesterday's magic has become today's commonplace. Ben Dooley was no longer present. In an electronic instant, without benefit of wand or incantation, he had flashed beyond reach of argument or appeal.

Slowly, McGonigle put the phone back in its cradle and turned around. His audience regarded him solemnly. He was aware of the reproachful gaze of Uncle Wilmer Kirby. Then he heard the voice of Bobo Strowger.

"Well boys," said Bobo cheerfully, "I guess that's that."

"But Dooley doesn't mean it," protested McGonigle. "He's got a quick temper. Always flying off the handle. Just kidding. He wouldn't fire me."

"Maybe he wouldn't," said Uncle Wilmer, gloomily, "but it sounds to me like he just did."

Uncle Wilmer trudged back to the platform. He whacked on the table to restore order.

"Fellas," he said. "Mr. McGonigle has been challenged to come up with a better deal. But it looks as if he's having a little trouble with his boss. Maybe if we let this ride for a few days..."

"Mr. Chairman." Blackjack Snead unfolded himself. "I have submitted a very generous offer which has been accepted by the executive of this club. I have guaranteed to supply you with a goalkeeper of professional calibre for your game tonight. My people want their answer now. Not tomorrow. Not the day after. Not next week, but *now*. I request that this meeting ratify our agreement immediately."

"All those in favour say aye!'" bawled Bobo Strowger.

The windows rattled to the resounding roar of confirmation.

"Against?" inquired Uncle Wilmer, hopefully.

One hand shot up.

"I'm agin it," announced Slewfoot.

Uncle Wilmer shook his head.

"Sorry, Slewfoot," he said. "Looks like you're outnumbered. Motion carried. Meeting's adjourned."

17

Mr. Wildgoose Returns a Favour

The annual Gold Cup Game was advertised to begin at eight-thirty that night, but the festivities actually got under way at about three o'clock in the afternoon when strange noises were heard from the hills north of Snowshoe Lake. Growing louder and clearer as they drew closer these sounds of invasion became identifiable as the honking of car horns, the clanking of cowbells, the bleating of bugles, and the bellowing of human voices raised in song. Soon three backfiring buses and a dozen cars bulging with delegates from Golden Valley swept down the main street with all horns blasting and all passengers roaring, "Hail, Hail, the Gang's All Here." On the side of each bus flapped a cotton banner with "Go-Go Old-timers" in letters of crimson.

Having shattered the afternoon peace and quiet of Snowshoe Lake, the invaders came tumbling out of their cars and buses into the snow of the arena parking lot and marched thirstily toward the Lakeshore. They were headed by a patriot thumping on a bass drum (filched from Salvation Army headquarters that morning) which served as the nucleus of a small but extremely noisy band. The instruments — cowbells, bugles, moose-calls, and even a set of bagpipes — created an ear-splitting din which attracted every small boy and resident dog from the uttermost suburbs of Snowshoe Lake. And so, with small boys jeering, dogs yapping, the band thumping, braying, clanking, whining, tootling, and booming, and the visitors insisting that the gang was indeed present, the annual Old-timer's Hockey Game rolled into its preliminary phases.

From the window of Emma Dinwoodie's room at the Lakeshore, Skates McGonigle viewed these festivities with every appearance of enjoyment. He chuckled when the man with the bass drum blundered into a snowbank. He slapped his knee when a dog fled howling from the bagpipes.

But this was merely a pose, assumed to deceive his companions. Inwardly, his soul was steeped in gloom.

"Dunno how you can be so cheerful," said Slewfoot.

"Mr. McGonigle just isn't the kind to go around with a long puss on account of a couple of bad breaks," Emma said. "Although heaven knows I wouldn't blame him. It was all my fault."

"I wish you wouldn't talk like that." McGonigle leaned forward and watched the whooping mob from Golden Valley charge into the beer parlour below. "Not your fault at all."

"It's true," she mourned. "If I hadn't been so smart and talked you into that stupid nomdayploom it wouldn't have happened."

"And I shouldn't have said you were my brother," declared Slewfoot. "Around this town that's enough to make you out a bum right off the bat."

"But we did it for the best." Emma brushed away a tear. "You know that, Skates. We were trying to help."

"Will you both stop talking foolish?" McGonigle turned away from the window. He gave Emma a little hug, which cheered her up immensely, and slapped Slewfoot on a shoulder. "You've both been good friends and you've both helped me a lot."

"We helped you get fired," said Emma.

McGonigle shook his head.

"I did that all by myself. Dooley was right. I gummed it up. Now I've got to ungum it."

"How do you figure to do that?" inquired Slewfoot. "How do you figure to get this club to go back on a deal they've already signed, when you can't offer 'em anything better."

"Better?" exclaimed Emma. "He can't offer 'em anything."

"Yeah," agreed Slewfoot. He turned to McGonigle again. "How do you figure to ungum a deal under them circumstances?"

"In my playing days," McGonigle replied stoutly, "I never quit until the game was over. And it wasn't over until they blew the siren and the referee picked up the puck."

"A spirit that does you credit," applauded Emma.

"But Skates, this game's over," Slewfoot insisted. "Didn't you hear that siren when your boss hung up on you?"

Emma turned a severe eye on Slewfoot.

"You quit trying to discourage Mr. McGonigle. Here he is trying to be cheerful, and we sit around moaning. He'll come up with something. Didn't you just hear him say it was up to him to ungum the situation? I'll bet his brain is working on it right now."

They gazed at McGonigle hopefully. McGonigle tried to look like a man whose brain is working.

"What you got in mind, Skates?" inquired Slewfoot.

"Ug," said McGonigle.

"Don't hurry him. Nobody can come up with ideas if somebody's snapping their fingers and saying what have you got in mind. It takes time."

"I have an idea myself," Slewfoot said. "Not that I'm much of a hand for ideas, and maybe it wouldn't work anyway," he added modestly, "but it come to me when I was thinking about that unbeatable goalkeeper who's going to play for us tonight. If we win, it's going to make Blackjack Snead a goldarn hero."

"So?" asked McGonigle.

"But suppose that unbeatable goalie doesn't show up, and we get licked again as usual? Won't that make a bum out of Blackjack Snead? Won't folks feel like running him out of town?"

"A beautiful thought," said Emma. She considered it for a moment. "But how are you going to fix it that Unbeatable Bates doesn't show up?"

"I've got a few bucks. So have you. We could pay him to get lost."

Mrs. Dinwoodie sniffed.

"The kind of fellow who would take our money to get lost is the kind who would take our money and show up anyway. And what could we do about it besides calling him a nasty man?"

"Everyone in town is betting on Snowshoe Lake to *win* this game," McGonigle pointed out. "Have you forgotten that? If that goalie doesn't show up everyone will lose his shirt."

"By gosh, you're right. I didn't figure it out that far."

"And who'd get the blame? Snead? No. It would be me. I'd be the one they would run out of town, and maybe they'd chase you out with me."

Emma gave Slewfoot a withering look.

"You and your bright ideas!"

"I guess I just ain't got the training for it," Slewfoot said. "Let's go downstairs and see what's going on."

Downstairs there was a great deal going on. When they descended into the lobby, they were engulfed by a roaring, cheerful, surging crowd. The old-timers had taken over, and in the North Country where the old-timers of every camp know the old-timers of all other camps in the ancient fraternity of adventurous and wandering men, this was the kind of joyful gathering where old feuds withered and old friendships bloomed anew.

They paraded in the streets, they gathered in the Legion Hall, they congregated in the curling club, but most of all they swarmed to the Lakeshore, where every old-timer knew that every other old-timer would turn up sooner or later. The Lakeshore's two beverage rooms — "beverage" being an Ontario euphemism for beer, with all its connotations of debauchery and sin — were in a state of cheerful uproar. Over in Ladies and Escorts the piper had been hoisted to a table top and was now going red in the face as he played "Road to the Isles" by unanimous request of an audience which insisted on providing vocal accompaniment, although very few knew the words; in any case, half a dozen choristers were already in tears, although it was not yet five o'clock.

Because Mrs. Dinwoodie qualified as a "Lady," which she resented, and Slewfoot automatically qualified as an "Escort," they became separated from McGonigle, who found himself surrounded by admirers who insisted on chivvying him into the Men's Beverage Room, where everyone wanted to buy him a beer and touch the hem of his garment.

From past experience, McGonigle knew that if he sat down at all, he would be expected to consume about four gallons of beer should he hope to escape without offending his admirers. So he pleaded a touch of liver trouble, shook every hand in sight, scribbled his name on every grimy envelope thrust in front of him for an autograph, and was slowly edging his way toward the street door, when an ancient, white-bearded man of spectacular baldness beckoned to him from a corner table.

When McGonigle approached, the old gentleman got to his feet. He beckoned McGonigle even closer, so close in fact that he breathed heavily into McGonigle's left ear.

"I want to talk to you," he said. "In private."

With that, he opened a door close by, and with sundry winks and jerks of his head, he indicated that McGonigle was to follow him. He led the way down a gloomy hall, opened another door and descended a flight of stairs into a basement room stacked high with cases of empties. There he turned and extended a bony hand.

"Name's Wildgoose," said the ancient, hoarsely. He regarded McGonigle through faded blue eyes. "Ring a bell?"

It was not a name easily forgotten.

"There was a Johnny Wildgoose."

"You remember him?"

"Played a season with me on the old Ramblers. Long time ago."

"Grandson," said old Mr. Wildgoose.

"He was a nice kid."

The old man nodded thoughtfully, groped in a pocket, and fished out a small tin of snuff. He wedged a large pinch of it beneath his upper lip.

"You was good to Johnny."

"No more'n anybody else."

"You was good to him. He always said. Johnny said you was the only man on that club was friendly, tried to help him along."

"Why shouldn't I? He was just a kid, away from home for the first time. I didn't do anything. Johnny had a couple of good years."

"Too light. Never made it. Got himself hurt and had to quit. But every time he wrote home he said you was good to him." The old man extended his hand again. "Can I say thanks?"

"Doesn't call for thanks. It's an honour for me to shake hands with Johnny's grandpa. What's he doing now? Where is he?"

"Out on the Coast. Runs a service station. Got kids of his own now."

"That's fine. You remember me to him, will you?"

"I'll tell him I saw you." The voice of old Mr. Wildgoose dropped to a whisper again. "You keep your mouth shut if I tell you something?"

"Depends. Why?"

"Won't tell you unless you give me your word you'll keep it to yourself."

"What can I lose? Okay."

"Cross your heart and hope to die?"

McGonigle held up his hand. "Word of honour, Mr. Wildgoose."

Mr. Wildgoose chewed reflectively on his wad of snuff.

"You bettin' on tonight's game?"

"Maybe."

"Snowshoe Lake supposed to be gettin' a new goalie. You bettin' on Snowshoe Lake?"

"Maybe."

"Don't," advised Mr. Wildgoose in a husky whisper.

He turned away and shuffled toward the stairs. McGonigle followed.

"You don't think it's a good bet?"

Mr. Wildgoose shook his head.

"Why?"

"They ain't going to get that new goalie."

"But he's on his way here now."

Mr. Wildgoose looked McGonigle in the eye.

"When that bus gets here," he said, again in the hoarse and conspiratorial whisper, "the goalie ain't going to be on it."

He was on the third step of the stairs when McGonigle said, "Why isn't he going to be on the bus?"

"I didn't say he isn't going to *be* on the bus," replied Mr. Wildgoose. "All I said was that he ain't going to be on it when the bus *gets* here. So, like I said, don't bet on Snowshoe Lake."

He proceeded up the stairs. McGonigle could get nothing more out of him. Old Mr. Wildgoose merely said, "Remember what you promised," before he went back into the beverage room. There he returned to his table and his companions from Golden Valley, who were now yowling "In the Evening by the Moonlight" with great feeling. Soon the quavery voice of Mr. Wildgoose joined the chorus. McGonigle realized that no further information could be expected.

McGonigle pushed his way through the crowd. Out on the street, he pondered.

Obviously, the Golden Valley crowd knew all about the prospective arrival of Unbeatable Bates. This was not surprising. Hockey fans are incurable blabbermouths and Snead's promise was public knowledge anyway. But it was equally obvious that Golden Valley had taken steps to meet the threat.

McGonigle's first impulse was to seek out Emma Dinwoodie and Slewfoot. It was merely an impulse, however. On the record, any help they might give would likely be disastrous. They would be much better off in the convivial atmosphere of Ladies and Escorts, hammering beer mugs on the table and beating time to "Road to the Isles."

He lowered his head against the north wind and set a course for Uncle Wilmer Kirby's store.

18

The Abduction
of Unbeatable Bates

About four o'clock that afternoon Uncle Wilmer decided to
pack it up. Business was far from brisk. The sounds of revelry
in the streets were becoming more than flesh and blood could
stand. And for the first time in his life he felt uncomfortable
in his own store.

"It's the lad," he told Happy Thorpe. "He's peeved about
what happened at the meeting."

"What did he say?"

"Nothing. That's the trouble. If he'd lose his temper and
yell at me and kick over a stack of snow shovels I'd feel better.
Then we could have a big argument and clear the air. But he
just doesn't say anything. He mopes."

"Didn't you explain to him?"

"Might as well explain to a wooden Indian. I told him the
sponsor deal was the best thing ever happened to hockey in
this town. He just gave me a look. I told him we didn't have
any choice, because McGonigle couldn't come up with a better deal. He just gave me another look and went down in the
basement. He's there now, checking stock. And moping."

"You can't get a word out of him?"

"Oh, I know what's bothering the boy. He's always wanted to play for the Blueshirts. And besides, he figures McGonigle got a raw deal."

As a matter of fact Uncle Wilmer was haunted by vague feelings of guilt in that direction himself. He could not get rid of a nagging suspicion that he had been fast-talked into something he was going to regret. And no matter how often he told himself that Skates McGonigle was the bumbling author of his own troubles, in the back of Uncle Wilmer's mind lurked an uneasy notion that there had been skulduggery in the snowbanks.

A great whoop-de-do outside heralded the arrival of another carload of reinforcements from Golden Valley. Uncle Wilmer went to the head of the basement stairs.

"Tim," he bawled. "Lock up any time you want. I'm going out."

He rejoined Happy Thorpe and struggled into his coat.

"After all," said Uncle Wilmer, "as president of the hockey club isn't it my duty to be over at the Lakeshore extending the hand of friendship?"

"Especially when every time you extend the hand of friendship somebody always sticks a bottle of beer in it," replied Mr. Thorpe. "As secretary of the club I think it's my duty to go with you."

They departed on their mission of welcome. Tim came up from the basement. Had he heard Uncle Wilmer's charge that he was moping over the hockey club decision he would have denied it. Silent he had been, and absorbed in thought, indisposed to exchange jolly quips about the new deal, but what Uncle Wilmer viewed as the mopes was nothing more than bewilderment.

It was true, as Uncle Wilmer said, that Tim Beckett had always wanted to play for the Blueshirts. Just as any youngster devoted to any sport has his individual hero, he gives his allegiance to one club. For Tim, that club had always been the Blueshirts. When he was a small boy, the first hockey sweater he ever found beneath the Christmas tree — in reply to Santa Claus letters fortified by prayer — had borne the Blueshirt crest. In any dreams in which he saw himself as a future big-league player, he always wore a Blueshirt uniform; anything else would have been unthinkable.

Even yet, brooding behind the counter, he could scarcely believe that the Bears had actually taken over the obscure Snowshoe Lake Hockey Club. Nor could he believe that from now on his own career would be determined by men in the Bears' organization, shadowy men of whom he had never heard and whom he might never see.

Through the frosty window he saw a big, burly man coming up the steps. The door opened.

"Mr. McGonigle!"

"Hi there, Beckett. Is this where you work?"

"I thought you'd gone back."

"I wouldn't go back without having a talk with you. Where's your uncle?"

"He went over to the Lakeshore. If you want to wait, I'll go look for him."

McGonigle shook his head.

"I need a car."

"Uncle Wilmer's car is parked out back. I'm sure he wouldn't mind letting you have it. Could I drive you somewhere?"

"Don't you have to mind store?"

"Uncle Wilmer said I could lock up. Not much business this afternoon anyway."

McGonigle considered.

"Can you keep things to yourself?"

"Yes, sir."

"I'm playing a hunch. I can't tell you anything. But I want to drive out along the highway and meet the afternoon bus."

"But it'll be here in fifteen minutes."

"I know."

Tim looked at him. Then he snapped the front-door lock.

"Okay, Mr. McGonigle."

He led the way out the back door and locked it. They got into Uncle Wilmer's car. The engine roared. The rear tires kicked up a cloud of snow. The car nosed down the alley and swung out into Main Street.

McGonigle glanced at his companion. He liked the way the boy accepted the situation. No questions. No probing. No doubt he was curious, but it didn't show.

"I'm sorry the way things turned out," McGonigle said. "I suppose you know I came up here to scout you."

"I heard."

"I talked to your mother last night."

"She told me."

The car sped past the Snowshoe Lake Mine, with its grey surface buildings, the ore dump blanketed with snow, the shaft house with its towering head and slanted roof. They skimmed toward the highway.

"What should I do, Mr. McGonigle?"

"What do you want to do?"

"I want to play hockey."

"For a living? For a career?"

"If I'm good enough."

McGonigle could see the boy's face in the mirror. Something hit him in the pit of the stomach. He was looking at himself a long time ago. Seventeen. Not much schooling. Small town. Never been on a plane, a train, or in a hotel. All he knew was hockey. And at that he knew he was pretty good. Better than most. His father had played, but didn't go very far. The old man had him on skates out on a backyard rink when he was five. Used to stand behind the boards in zero weather to watch him play with the school team; got into a fight with another kid's father one night when the other kid clobbered him from behind.

There wasn't much money. The old man worked in a sawmill. A screaming, draughty place, cold in winter, sweltering hot in summer, but he said he liked the smell of sawdust and fresh-cut boards. Worked hard right up to the time pneumonia caught up with him one spring. In hockey, he saw escape for his boy.

"You've got what it takes, Danny," he used to say. "If you play your cards right you'll make it. But don't ever play for nothin'. Make 'em put up the dough. Don't ever take the first offer. What the hell, they make money outta you, you're entitled to your share. Be tough about money, they'll respect you all the more."

It wasn't easy. It wasn't easy to fight your way into the big league and it wasn't easy to hold out for more money all the time, to squeeze them, especially when you loved the game so much you would have paid *them* to let you play, and they knew it. But the old man was right. To the fans and the players, hockey was a sport, one of the great games; to the owners it was a business. They took in as much as they could at the box office and paid out as little as they could get away with.

A business. You had to find that out. And yet to McGonigle it had always been something more. A craft. A religion. A way of living. And where was all the money now? Where was it gone? And where was he going?

Now this boy was asking him, "What should I do?"

McGonigle said, "If you stay in school, if you go on to college, what will you be?"

"A mining engineer."

"A good one?"

"I think so. I've been on some prospecting trips with my father."

"Would you rather be a mining engineer than anything else in the world?"

Tim shook his head. "No."

"What, then?"

"A hockey player."

"Why? The money? The crowds? People making a fuss over you? Your picture in the papers?"

"That stuff doesn't mean much to me. It's just this. I enjoy playing hockey so much that I don't get much fun out of it any more when the fellows playing against me — I hardly know how to put it..."

"When they aren't very good."

"That's right. I'd like to play against a really good junior club some time. If I could skate with their forwards and beat their defence — boy, that would be something! And then when I get older, if I could make it in the NHL, be good enough to hold my own with the best in the world, well, what more could a fellow want?"

They were out on the open highway west of town now. Away ahead, McGonigle could see a car parked on the south side of the road, just short of a curve, near a clump of evergreens.

"Would you know by the licence plate if a car was from Golden Valley?"

"Plates over there are in a J-series. Ours are in S."

"Take a look at this one as we go past."

There were three men sitting in the parked car. Tim took his eyes off the road for a moment and glanced at the plate.

"Golden Valley car. I saw it in town earlier. Belongs to one of the hockey crowd."

"Fine," said McGonigle. "I think my hunch is working out." They left the parked car behind. "When you see the bus coming, we'll stop and wait for it."

"Right."

Still no questions.

"The point is," McGonigle said, "if you've got an ability — a talent — like playing the violin, maybe, or painting pictures, or making people laugh or doctoring or making things grow, even; if you've got something special and that's all you want to do, because it doesn't seem like work, why that's what you should do, no matter what anyone says because you won't be happy doing anything else."

"But what if Mr. Snead moves me away? They say I'll always have to play wherever the Bears send me."

"Later on, if you want to play pro hockey, you'll have to be in some big-league organization. And you'll have to play where they want you to play. That's how you get experience. On the farm clubs. Then maybe someday you make it. Or if they make a deal for you, and you have to go somewhere else in a trade or a sale, that's what you have to do, because that's the way things are. You have to understand that right at the beginning. Once you sign, you'll never again be your own master unless you're good enough and big enough to write your own ticket."

McGonigle peered through the windshield. Away ahead he saw a bulky object in a mist of snow.

"How about school?" asked Tim.

"It's a tough deal all around," said McGonigle. "But don't drop school. Go to college. They'll tell you it can't be done, but it can. Apps did it. More and more of the good players do it every year. So when they're through with hockey or hockey's through with them they've got something. Look at me, kid. Grade nine. What good's grade nine nowadays? Better than nothing, I'll admit. But not much."

"You think I should give up hockey?"

McGonigle shook his head.

"If you were just ordinary it would be different. But you're not. You've got to give yourself your chance. If you did something else, even if you wound up a millionaire, you wouldn't be happy. All the rest of your life you'd feel you turned your back on something you really wanted. You'd wake up at night wondering what it would have been like playing in the NHL. And you'd never know."

The bus was speeding toward them.

"Pull over," said McGonigle.

The car slowed down, came to a stop. McGonigle got out and went across the road. He flagged down the bus. The driver was sore. He glared down at McGonigle.

"I don't pick up no passengers out here."

"Who asked you?" McGonigle swung himself on board. A handful of people. A couple of old men dozing in the back seat. A bovine Indian woman with some black-eyed youngsters.

And Unbeatable Charlie Bates, reading a paperback.

Lean, lanky, flap-eared. A long jaw, a face seamed with scars. A nose that had been broken many times. Bleak blue eyes peering out from under the scar tissue. A crooked grin.

"Skates!" he yelled.

"Hi, Charlie. Get your gear."

"Skates McGonigle!" marvelled the Unbeatable. "Where'd you come from?"

McGonigle hauled the suitcase off the rack.

"I came out to meet you."

Unbeatable Bates scrambled out of the seat, reached for a duffel bag bulging with his skates and gear.

"Skates," he said, "I don't know what it's all about but you must know what you're doin'. Lead the way."

McGonigle took a bill from his wallet. He shook hands with the bus driver.

"Farther down the road," he said, "you'll be flagged down again. Some fellows waiting to meet my friend, here, to drive him into town. But he won't be on the bus, see."

"That figures."

"What you're going to tell 'em is that he never *was* on the bus. Right?"

"Missed his plane, huh?"

"That's what must have happened. His name's Bates. He missed his plane. You never saw him."

The driver slipped the bill into his jacket pocket.

"Never saw him, never heard of him. Never saw you either," he told McGonigle. "Bye now."

They got off. The door slammed shut. The bus roared, lurched forward, zoomed off down the highway.

Unbeatable Bates looked quizzically at McGonigle.

"It's been a long time. All of a sudden the bus stops in the middle of Baffin Land and who climbs aboard but Skates McGonigle. What gives?"

"They take their hockey seriously up here, Charlie. Some fellows down the road figured they'd give you a little personal welcome, just to be sure you wouldn't make it to the game tonight."

"You mean shanghai me?"

"Something like that."

"Betting money floatin' around in large quantities?"

"I hear tell." Tim swung open the car door. "Get in and meet my friend Tim Beckett."

"Hi, kid." The Unbeatable climbed in with the duffel bag.

"And make careful note of the name, because some day you'll want to tell your grandchildren all about the first time you met up with him."

The Unbeatable glanced at McGonigle with a flicker of inquiry.

"A comer?"

McGonigle nodded.

Tim said, "It's an honour to meet you, Mr. Bates."

The Unbeatable was gratified. "Two reception committees. Folks calling me mister before I even hit town. Great big warm-hearted North Country!"

The car swung around and headed back toward Snowshoe Lake.

"Where do you want to go now?" Tim asked. "The Lakeshore?"

"That's right." McGonigle chuckled. He nudged the Unbeatable. "Those Golden Valley boys are going to look pretty stunned when we walk in."

Then the great idea hit him.

Why *should* Unbeatable Bates walk into the Lakeshore?

"Wait a minute," he said. "Hold everything. The Lakeshore is no place for an honoured guest. Too crowded. Too noisy. Too many Golden Valley fans waving their money around, getting bets down on their hockey team."

"What's wrong with that?" inquired the Unbeatable. "Let 'em bet. I'm gonna shut 'em out."

"That's what I mean. If you show up it'll spoil their fun. They won't put up a nickel. Let's go some place quiet."

"Where, Mr. McGonigle?"

"Slewfoot Shannon's place." McGonigle grinned at Unbeatable Bates. "You'll like it there."

19

The Unbeatable Finds Spiritual Help

As has been said before, in the North Country a man who locks his door brands himself as a mean, inhospitable curmudgeon, lacking trust in the human race. Slewfoot Shannon was no curmudgeon, and while his innocent faith in his fellow men had cost him sums of money from time to time, he was proud to say that the open-door policy had never cost him so much as a pound of coffee.

"There's always an extra bunk, wood behind the stove, and grub on the shelf for anybody wants to drop in whether I'm here or not," he once said, "I'd be mortified if any friend of mine had a fight with his wife or wanted to sleep off a drunk and come here looking for refuge and found the door locked. It wouldn't be right."

"Nice little hideout," said Unbeatable Bates, approvingly, when he looked the place over. "Like you say, Skates, there's no point in giving the enemy a peek when you've got an ace in the hole."

"I'll go uptown and tell Slewfoot he has a guest. Make yourself at home." McGonigle checked the food supply.

"There's bacon and eggs if you get hungry. And beans, of course. And moose steak."

"Don't worry about me. Just tell Snead I'm in town, so he won't get frantic because I wasn't on the bus. And look, he was going to pay me a hundred bucks. Tell him to plunk it down on Snowshoe Lake at the best odds he can get."

"The odds should be pretty good by now."

"Get a few bob down yourself."

McGonigle shook his head.

"I'll bet on anything except hockey. Some day I'll tell you why."

"But this one you can't lose. It's a lock. Those hamburgers can't beat me. I'll shut 'em out."

"I wouldn't be surprised. But even if we were playing against the Old Ladies' Home, I still wouldn't bet on a hockey game. Matter of principle."

"You could make a hatful on this game." The Unbeatable sat down on a bunk. "I'm going to grab a little shut-eye. Come game time I'll be rarin' to go."

On the way back uptown Tim said, "Why won't you bet on hockey games, Skates?"

"Because the more you know about hockey the more you realize what a tricky game it is. There's always a night when the cellar team clobbers the leader."

Around the Lakeshore and the Legion Hall, as more cars from Golden Valley roared honking into town, the atmosphere of holiday and merriment had heightened. When the car stopped in front of the Lakeshore McGonigle said, "Thanks for your help, lad."

"I'm glad there was something I could do. And thank *you*."

"For what? All I did was gum things up, like Ben Dooley said."

"I'm thanking you for everything you told me. And for what you tried to do for me. And, Skates..."

"Yeah?"

"I think it's mighty big of you to help Blackjack Snead the way you did. If it hadn't been for you, Unbeatable Bates might be halfway to Golden Valley by now, and Mr. Snead would be in a lot of trouble."

"I didn't do it for Snead. He could still be in trouble."

Tim brightened.

"You mean there's still a chance?"

"I never give up, kid," said McGonigle.

He went into the hotel where he was immensely cheered to see Blackjack Snead surrounded by a noisily belligerent group, all members of the Snowshoe Lake Hockey Club. Uncle Wilmer, by virtue of his office, appeared to be the spokesman, although his was not the only voice raised in wrath. It was merely the loudest.

"You gave us your solemn word of honour," bellowed Uncle Wilmer, wagging a finger under Snead's nose. "You *promised*! You said you'd have a ringding snapper of a goalie for us — Unbeatable Charlie Bates, no less, and you said he'd be here on the afternoon bus. Where is he?"

"That's what we want to know!" yelped Happy Thorpe. "What happened?"

"We trusted you," howled Fergy MacAllister. "Do you realize we've been betting like crazy, just because we were stupid enough to believe you? What are you trying to do to us? This town will be in hock for the next forty years, we'll take such a beating."

"I tell you he phoned me from the airport," yelled Blackjack Snead above the din. "Can I help it if he missed the bus? Will you wait until you're hurt before you holler. I tell you, Bates never missed a game in his life. He'll *be* here, even if he has to walk."

"In that case he won't show up until four o'clock tomorrow morning," shouted Happy Thorpe. "A fat lot of good he'll do us then."

"Unbeatable Bates will be in that goal tonight."

A fat man named Caspar Yollik approached. He wore a festoon of Golden Valley ribbons and he waved a fistful of ten-dollar bills.

"It's going begging, boys. Can't find anybody willing to risk a buck. You fellows all lost your enthusiasm?"

They regarded him sourly and in silence.

"We're giving odds. Two to one."

No one reached for a wallet.

"Five to two?" said Yollik, hopefully.

Uncle Wilmer looked at Blackjack Snead.

"If you're so all-fired sure," he challenged, "why don't you grab some of that."

"I didn't bring more than a couple of hundred with me," said Snead. "And I already got it down."

"Tell you what I'll do," said Caspar Yollik, the fat man. "I know I'm crazy but it runs in the family. Three to one. Anybody who'll pass that up must be even crazier than me."

McGonigle gulped. It was true, as he told Tim, that he had long clung to the principle that anyone who wagered money on a hockey game was lacking in sense. But now he began to waver.

Perhaps, he told himself, there were times when a man owed it to himself to abandon a principle that was normally sound. If the fat man knew that Unbeatable Charlie Bates was at that moment safely and snugly ensconced in Slewfoot Shannon's cabin, it was highly unlikely that he would be waving a fistful of money with such carefree abandon. And it was certain that he would never be so rash as to tempt catastrophe by mentioning odds of three to one. But McGonigle knew what the fat man did not know. The presence of Unbeatable Bates removed the element of risk. While a foolish man might gamble, a prudent man would invest. This could be regarded as an investment, based on solid information, which no sensible person should ignore.

His hand crept toward his hip pocket.

"Oh come on now." Caspar Yollik flicked the sheaf of bills with his thumb. "It's a sin to pass up odds like that. A downright sin. What's happened to this town? Ain't there any sports left in Snowshoe Lake?"

McGonigle fished out his wallet. It contained five twenties and a crumpled dollar bill.

"Like you say," he told the fat man, "a fellow would have to be crazy to pass up three to one. I'll take a hundred of that."

"Man, aren't you the reckless one!" chortled Yollik. He began peeling off bills with great dexterity. Uncle Wilmer grabbed McGonigle by the arm and drew him aside.

"Look, Mac," he said, "I know the odds are tempting, but you've never seen our goalie. Even ten years ago we called him the Human Sieve. Since then he's been drinking a bucket of beer a day and he's up to two hundred and forty pounds. Can't even bend over to put on his own skates. He's big. I'll give him that. And he's brave. But that's because pucks don't hit him. They go past him."

"Maybe Bates will show up," said McGonigle.

He went over to the desk with the fat man, and they left their money with Al, the clerk, who was presiding as official stakeholder and recorder of transactions. Caspar Yollik shook McGonigle warmly by the hand, told Al that he would present himself immediately after the game to collect his winnings, and departed in search of other victims. Al wagged his head sorrowfully.

"Them that has, gets," he remarked. "That fellow Yollik got rid of some moose pasture last fall for eighty thousand bucks and he's still making money. Somebody should have warned you, Mr. McGonigle."

"About what?"

"The new goalie didn't show up," groaned Al. "Up until the five o'clock bus came in, our boys were taking all the Golden Valley money in sight. The bus came in — no goalie. Now everybody's sick. They shoulda told you."

"I'd bet more if I had it," said McGonigle, to Al's unbounded astonishment.

He went in search of Mrs. Dinwoodie and Slewfoot and found them in Ladies and Escorts, looking so cheerful that they could easily have been mistaken for visitors from Golden Valley.

"Where you been?" Emma Dinwoodie was beaming. "You hear the good news?"

"I heard that Unbeatable Bates didn't show up."

"You heard correct," said Slewfoot, with a grin. "I was there when the bus came in. Wouldn't have missed it for anything. Reception committee all waiting in front of the hotel. Blackjack Snead, looking modest and proud like a man who just had a mountain named after him, Bobo Strowger, Uncle Wilmer, Fergy MacAllister, half the hockey club, everybody with his hand out and his mouth open ready to shake hands with Unbeatable Bates and sing 'For He's a Jolly Good Fellow.' The bus stops, the door opens, Indian lady and four kids get out. Smile disappears off Snead's face. 'You got another passenger?' he says to the driver. 'Two more,' says the driver, 'but they're gettin' out farther up the road.' 'But where's Unbeatable Bates?' Bobo wants to know. 'Never heard of him,' says the driver. He shuts the door, away goes the bus. Everybody looks at Snead. 'I can't understand it,' he says. 'We're ruined,' moans Happy Thorpe. 'We trusted you, Snead,' says Fergy MacAllister, 'and now look what you've done to us.' 'There must be some explanation,' says Snead. 'There'd better be,' I pipes up, just to be helpful. So we all go back into the hotel and the last I saw Snead was still trying to square himself and makin' no headway."

"Looked like he'd been sandbagged," declared Emma, with great satisfaction. "It would have done your heart good."

"It does," said McGonigle.

Slewfoot observed that there was another bright side to the matter, in addition to the discomfiture of Snead. Neither he nor Mrs. Dinwoodie had been foolish enough to bet any money, in which they were luckier than most. On the dark side was the certainty of a Snowshoe Lake hockey defeat, with financial loss to the citizenry.

"Until next payday," said Slewfoot, "this is going to be the most busted town in Canada."

"Fellow upstairs named Yollik," said McGonigle. "Gave me three to one. I bet a hundred on Snowshoe Lake." He extracted the dollar bill from his wallet. "It leaves me a buck. I'll buy you both a beer."

Mrs. Dinwoodie cocked her head on one side and regarded McGonigle with deep interest. Slewfoot slapped his right ear and commented on a touch of deafness that had been bothering him of late. It wasn't so much that he couldn't hear, but that he kept hearing things that didn't make sense.

"Up to now," Mrs. Dinwoodie observed, "I've been kind of sorry for you, Mr. McGonigle. Seemed to me that you were a nice, well-meaning man who got into trouble because he was just naturally unlucky. Now I'm beginning to wonder. Maybe it's because you're just plain stupid."

McGonigle leaned forward.

"Slewfoot," he said in an impressive whisper, "you have a guest."

"Me? How come?"

"He needed a place to stay. Some place quiet, where people wouldn't bother him. He's holed up in your cabin now. I told him you wouldn't mind."

"Course I don't mind. Anybody wants to bunk in at my..." His mouth fell open. His eyes bulged. "No!"

McGonigle nodded.

"Unbeatable Bates?"

"Glory be!" exclaimed Emma. "You son-of-a-gun! I take it all back. About you being stupid, I mean."

"Aside from Tim Beckett, we're the only ones who know. And out in the lobby that fellow Yollik is still begging people to take his money."

Slewfoot got up in such haste that he nearly upset his beer.

"McGonigle," he said, "I don't know how you swung it and I'm sure looking forward to hearing the details, but I want to find that Yollik character before he runs out of dough or comes to his senses. Wait here."

"Wait?" said Mrs. Dinwoodie. "Don't be greedy. I'm coming with you."

Few cabins in the North Country were better built to afford shelter from the stormy blasts of winter than the humble domicile of Slewfoot Shannon. But even Slewfoot would have been forced to admit that its cultural resources were limited.

There was a battery radio which hadn't worked since an evening in October when Slewfoot had responded to a political speech by hurling the set against the wall. There was a deck of cards which lacked the ace of spades and the queen of diamonds. Unbeatable Charlie Bates discovered this when he tried to while away the time with a game of solitaire.

There was Slewfoot's fiddle, but one string was gone, and the Unbeatable couldn't play the fiddle anyway. As for literature, the Shannon library consisted of one mail-order catalogue, a copy of the Ontario Department of Mines report for 1923, a paperback mystery novel from which some fiend had removed the last three chapters, and a dozen tattered volumes of a quaint publication called *Ghost and Ghoul Comic Book.*

Having refreshed himself by a nap and fortified himself against the rigours of the evening ahead by a meal of bacon and eggs, Unbeatable Bates relaxed in a battered wicker chair, with his feet in the oven. A case of beer bottles had attracted his lively interest but investigation revealed that all the bottles were empty. And when his wandering glance fell upon an earthenware jug beneath the bunk he hauled it from its hiding place in a spirit of curiosity rather than hope. But when he hefted it his eyes brightened. The jug sloshed. He extracted the cork and sniffed.

The sharp, powerful, penetrating fragrance of Slewfoot Shannon's own private brew stung his nostrils. A fermentation of potatoes and raisins, generously strengthened by a few jolts of aged dandelion wine to add body and flavour, the liquid in the jug fairly sizzled with potency. Unbeatable Bates took another long and hearty sniff.

"Boyohboyohboy!" sighed the Unbeatable, gratefully. "I have struck oil."

He found a tin cup on a shelf. He put the cup on the table, carefully tilted the jug. There was a pleasant gurgle as he filled the cup. Slewfoot Shannon's own brew was a muddy amber in colour, and there was a wickedly bubbling foam which subsided into froth.

The Unbeatable took a cautious sip. His gullet was scorched and his stomach caught fire but the effect diminished by the time the stuff got to his toes. He stepped over to the water bucket, found another cup, made a judicious mixture. Another sip. Then a hearty gulp. A few tears spurted from his eyes but he was rewarded by a vast inner glow.

"Just what I needed," said Unbeatable Charlie Bates. "I'll shut 'em out tonight."

20

The Unbeatable Reports for Duty

By six o'clock, Caspar Yollik had gleefully accepted a two-thousand-dollar bet from Emma Dinwoodie and a five-hundred-dollar contribution from Slewfoot. Encouraged by this show of confidence, half a dozen of Snowshoe Lake's more devout optimists dug into their risk capital and resumed the betting that had come to an abrupt halt with the arrival of the bus.

Just why their faith had been miraculously restored they couldn't say. Common sense was against it. But a few courageous souls reasoned that if Skates McGonigle thought Snowshoe Lake had a chance he must have divined possibilities which were not apparent to ordinary mortals. After all, if he didn't know hockey, who else did?

As for Blackjack Snead, huddled in the lobby phone booth where he used up a fistful of quarters on long-distance calls, McGonigle let him sweat it out. Snead was in disgrace. He had made extravagant promises and had failed to deliver. The popularity of Bobo Strowger was also at a low ebb.

"Why blame me?" he protested. "I didn't promise any hot-shot goalie."

"You talked us into a deal with that highbinder," said Uncle Wilmer, glowering. "And the worst of it is, we're stuck with it. After tonight's game the club will be so broke we'll need all the help Snead's outfit can give us."

It was Happy Thorpe's considered opinion that Snead had conned them from the beginning.

"Never had any intention of getting us a goalie, least of all a goalie as good as Unbeatable Bates. He suckered us into this. Did it on purpose to back us into a corner. Now we can't get out."

Mr. Thorpe claimed a profound distrust of Blackjack Snead from the moment he laid eyes on the rascal. "In my business," he said, "you learn to size people up." But just how his melancholy profession developed an instinct for judging character, Mr. Thorpe did not bother to explain.

Slewfoot prevailed upon Uncle Wilmer to provide transportation back to the cabin. He had promised Emma and McGonigle a feed of moose steak and home-baked beans.

"Glad to oblige," said Uncle Wilmer, "as long as you don't offer me a drink." As the car lurched through the snowdrifts Slewfoot protested the reflection on his personal poteen. It was, he insisted, based on an old family recipe handed down from generation to generation of Shannons, all of whom imbibed it as a morning and evening tonic, with an occasional restorative jolt during the day. They had all lived to be ninety-five.

"The batch I uncorked last time you come to see me was a mite green," he explained. "Hadn't set long enough. I shouldn't have opened it."

"Maybe," grunted Uncle Wilmer, "but I don't care to risk it again. If I'm going to have the top of my head blown off I'd rather have it done by a jealous husband."

"A nice way to go," Emma Dinwoodie approved. "Messy, but manly."

When they reached the cabin Slewfoot insisted that Uncle Wilmer come inside for a moment.

"Got something to show you." He opened the door.

"Good grief!" said Emma.

In shocked silence McGonigle and Slewfoot stared at the snoring figure on the bunk.

"Looks like you had a visitor," said Uncle Wilmer.

"That ain't no visitor," Slewfoot confessed mournfully "That's a guest."

Uncle Wilmer sniffed. "Overcome by hospitality."

McGonigle sat down heavily. "This is all I needed," he groaned. Emma gave him a consoling pat on the shoulder.

"Brace up, Mr. McGonigle," she said. "It could be worse. At least he's alive. I can hear him snoring."

Uncle Wilmer inspected the slumbering guest.

"Stranger to these parts. Who is he, Slewfoot?"

Slewfoot looked into the empty tin cup. He picked up the jug and tested it for weight.

"All my fault," he muttered. "I shoulda remembered. The minute McGonigle told me where he was I shoulda hustled right home and collared that jug."

"Okay, okay," said Uncle Wilmer. "Why is everybody looking so stunned and grieved? So the guy got into your potato tonic. Serves him right for bein' so nosy. After he sleeps it off he'll feel awful but he'll recover in four or five days and it'll be a good lesson to him."

"But we're the ones who're going to pay for it," said Mrs. Dinwoodie. "That object on the bunk is Unbeatable Charlie Bates."

The resurrection of Unbeatable Bates was not achieved without resorting to heroic measures.

They shook him, they slapped him, they doused him with cold water, they took him outside and walked him around in the cold night air, they thrust his head into a snowbank, they applied icicles to the back of his neck. Emma Dinwoodie busied herself making strong coffee. By the time the coffee was ready Unbeatable Bates had his eyes open and was making anguished sounds of protest. After the second cup he mumbled inquiries as to where he was and what was going on. After the third cup he recognized McGonigle.

"Sorry, Skates," he muttered. "First time it's happened in eight years, believe me. Only had two snorts of the stuff. Must have been poisoned."

"I resent that, mister," said Slewfoot. "Grew the potatoes myself. The water came from my own spring. And the dandelions was the best crop we had in a coon's age. Brewer's yeast. But you musta took it on an empty stomach, that's what happened. An empty stomach." He shook his head.

"I'll be perfectly all right." Unbeatable Bates got to his feet, swaying. "Came to play goal; I'll play goal. Shut 'em out. Not one goal."

He spied a broom in a corner, seized it and took up a position in front of the bunk, crouching.

"Come in from the wing and try for the top corner."

McGonigle lobbed the tin cup. The Unbeatable swung mightily with the broom, and fanned. After they picked him up and propped him in the wicker chair he complained that it wasn't fair to use two pucks.

"I'll put on another pot of coffee," said Emma. "And you men take him outside and walk him around some more. Nothing like good cold winter air to clear the head."

"But *my* head is clear as a bell," objected Uncle Wilmer. "And it's fifteen below out there."

"Bundle up warm," she advised. "But don't fetch him back until he begins turning blue."

Outside, they walked the Unbeatable around. He responded so remarkably to the cold night air that he soon insisted he had never felt better. But when they released his elbows to test his ability to stand up by himself he pitched headlong into a snowbank. They picked him up, brushed off the snow and walked him around the cabin again.

"I got an idea," said Uncle Wilmer.

"It had better be a doozer."

"It come to me this afternoon when it looked like this here goalie wasn't going to show up. Now this here Old-timers' Game, it's exhibition hockey..."

"Oh no," said McGonigle.

"The rules ain't very strict. About who plays, I mean. There's a lot of give and take. As long as a man is over thirty-five and willing to play for us..."

"No dice. I've been out of the game for years."

"Look at it this way. You're going to get the blame anyway. You know that. What you did, you did for the best, that's for sure. But the way it turned out nobody's going to give you credit for a good try."

"Look, I get all out of puff just bending over to tie my shoelaces. I haven't skated in years. I couldn't help anybody no matter how hard I tried."

"It was just an idea," Uncle Wilmer said, with resignation. "But I guess you're right. You do look pretty pudgy. Too bad. Because I don't think this fellow is going to be worth a hoot in goal."

"You talking about me?" demanded Unbeatable Bates. "What do you mean I won't be worth a hoot in goal?" He shook himself free and glared at them belligerently. "I can play goal in my sleep better'n anybody you've got in this neck of the woods."

Uncle Wilmer sighed.

"I'm going to tell Bobo to put your name on the players' list anyway," he told McGonigle. "It sure can't do any harm."

"It won't do you any good either. Because I won't play. It's out of the question."

"One of our fellows came down with the flu yesterday. Hardrock Valenti. His uniform would just about fit you."

"Nothing doing!" shouted McGonigle. "You don't know what you're asking. I'd only make a fool of myself. Besides, it would probably kill me."

"You might change your mind," said Uncle Wilmer, mildly. "Any way you look at it, we're in trouble."

"Who's in trouble?" asked Unbeatable Bates. "What are we doing out here anyway?" His teeth were chattering. "Where's the rink? Let's go!"

At half-past seven that evening Blackjack Snead conceded defeat. Up to the last minute he clung to his faith in the Unbeatable. The goalie, he insisted, was bound to show up. Bates would never let him down. But finally, with the arena filling up, the Golden Valley music makers creating a joyful uproar, and the dressing rooms crowded with old-time hockey players, Snead had to admit that it would be a good idea to dress another goalie.

"And that," said Bobo, "is going to be a problem."

The Human Sieve, it appeared, was miffed.

He sat in Bobo's office, scowling and fully clad.

"Aw come off it, Enrico," begged Strowger. "Don't be like that. We need you."

"I was good enough to play goal last year and the year before that. I should have been good enough to play goal *this* year."

"But you are. We're asking you. Holy smoke, Enrico, don't go getting hurt feelings, just because there was some talk of another goalie."

"It was more than talk," growled the Sieve. "Just because the other guy let you down, now all of a sudden I'm good enough. Don't you think I got no pride?"

Bobo sighed. He went into the dressing room.

"Some of you fellows go and talk to him," he begged. "As if we didn't have enough trouble, now the Sieve is up on his high horse and says he won't dress. His feelings are hurt."

"He's *got* to dress," howled a defence player. "You think we're going out there without anybody in goal? He just wants to be coaxed."

Three of them clumped into the office and went to work on the Sieve. They appealed to his pride. He alone stood between Snowshoe Lake and catastrophe. Forget about the nine goals that got by him last year. Nobody blamed him. They appealed to his loyalty. Every hockey fan in Snowshoe Lake was out there waiting to see him skate out and take his accustomed place between the posts. It wouldn't be an Old-timers Game without him.

"Fine time to ask me," muttered the Sieve, beginning to relent. "Nobody with any pride wants to be asked at the last minute."

There was a great roar from the dressing room.

"What's going on out there?" Bobo opened the door. Old-timers in various stages of undress were crowding around Uncle Wilmer and a lanky, lantern-jawed stranger with a crooked nose. The stranger seemed a little dazed and his complexion was of a greenish pallor as if he had just survived a few weeks in a damp cellar.

"Here he is, boys," roared Uncle Wilmer. "Here's the man we've been waitin' for. Unbeatable Charlie Bates!"

The Unbeatable smiled amiably as he acknowledged the greetings of his new comrades. No one noticed that he didn't utter a word. The reason was simple. He couldn't. Some may have observed that his eyes lacked expression to the point of vacancy, and some may have thought it odd that he was swaying a little. But no one was actually concerned until Bobo

Strowger charged in with outstretched hand, whooping, "Man, am I ever glad to see you. Where you been?" and Uncle Wilmer released the goalie's arm. It was then that Unbeatable Bates fell flat on his face on the dressing-room floor.

"Holy smoke, he's fainted!" yelped Bobo. "It must be the heat."

They hauled the Unbeatable to his feet, hoisted him onto the rubbing table, and revived him with a whiff of ammonia. He sat up, gasping. Blackjack Snead hurried into the dressing room just in time to hear him say, "What happened to Skates McGonigle?"

"Bates!"

Snead gaped at the blinking goalie, then at Bobo, then at Uncle Wilmer.

"Where did he come from? What's wrong with him?"

"He was out at Slewfoot Shannon's place," explained Uncle Wilmer. "He's a little under the weather but he says he's going to be all right."

"McGonigle," mumbled the Unbeatable.

"What about McGonigle?"

"Took me off the bus. Where's my pads? I'll shut 'em out."

"What a lowdown, despicable, underhanded trick!" roared Snead. "McGonigle took you off that bus and got you plastered. I knew it. I knew there was dirty work somewhere. McGonigle did this to put me behind the eight ball." He turned to Bobo. "What are you waiting for? Get his clothes off. Get him into a uniform."

"But Blackjack, the guy doesn't look well."

"I promised you a goalie, didn't I? And here he is. I kept my part of the bargain and I want everybody to know it. Get him out there. Drunk or sober, he's still better than any other goalie you'll find in these parts."

"I don't think it was all McGonigle's fault," ventured Uncle Wilmer. "I think he meant well."

"Don't give me that. You heard what Bates said. Took him off the bus. Shanghaied."

"That's what they were trying to do. Very word McGonigle used. Tryin' to shanghai me, that's what McGonigle said."

"Hear that?" bawled Snead.

"McGonigle just figured to hide him out for a while, but the poor feller got into some of Slewfoot's homebrew," Uncle Wilmer explained. "Like dynamite. Especially on an empty stomach."

"Don't tell me it was an accident. A lousy, unprincipled trick." Snead turned to the gaping old-timers. "Boys," he said. "I'm sorry. But you'll have to admit it was no fault of mine. I did my best. And if you get licked tonight you'll know who to blame." He raised a condemnatory forefinger. "McGonigle!"

Bobo turned to the trainer.

"Give him another whiff of ammonia to clear his head. Get him into a uniform." He pointed at the stick boy. "You! Go on up to the cafe and get a gallon of black coffee."

"Won't do no good," said Uncle Wilmer. "He's already had a gallon. Every time you move him he sloshes."

"Don't worry about me," said Unbeatable Bates, grandly. He swung himself off the dressing table. They caught him before he hit the floor. They propped him up on a bench. "Help me on with my pads. Put a pair of skates on me. Get me out on the ice, aim me at the goal and give me a shove. I'll shut 'em out."

21

The Great Old-timers' Game

It was the considered opinion of Bramwell K. Peabody, known in the old days of the mining country as The Cobalt Kid, that the great game of hockey had been regulated out of all resemblance to the sport he remembered as a lad. He was fond of recalling the gay old times when the rinks were spattered with gore; when the Silver Seven and the Renfrew Millionaires beat each other's brains out and stole each other's players with no respect for ethics; when clubs and players, in short, did pretty much as they pleased. And so, when he concluded that modern hockey was being strangled by rules and regulations, Mr. Peabody founded and financed the annual Old-timers' Hockey Game, dedicated to the proposition that things were managed better in the old days.

At first, it was his notion that the annual contest should be played under old rules — seven men, including a rover, and no substitutions allowed. This experiment turned out to be impractical because the seven old-time hockey players all collapsed midway through the second period. It was agreed that the modern game had some merit, and conditions were revised. But the big feature remained. No residence rule. The community ingenious enough to round up a winning lineup was entitled to its reward, and no questions asked.

Mr. Peabody looked upon his work and found it good. As an expression of defiance toward constituted authority in the field of sport, the Old-timers' Hockey Game was unique. Mr. Peabody retired to California, satisfied that he would be favourably remembered in the North Country at least once a year.

Although some people cherish a fond belief that there is nothing like good clean sport to foster goodwill among men — as witness the benign atmosphere of brotherly love which prevails year after year at the Olympic Games, with its "freedom from petty squabbling"— the truth of the matter is that there is nothing like a lively sports feud to set otherwise sane communities at each other's throats.

As Uncle Wilmer Kirby put it the very first year Golden Valley won a ball game over Snowshoe Lake, on a close call at home plate in the twelfth inning: "You never really know how many genuine skunks there are in any town until that town comes up against you in a friendly game of anything."

The annual Old-timers' Game, with its atmosphere of carnival and combat, had always been a major break in the monotony of the North Country winter. All the simmering rivalries and vendettas between the two towns came to a head. Every time one was victorious the other was plunged into bitterness and despair, muttering charges of skulduggery.

Referees, invariably imported from distant centres, invariably found themselves assailed as optically defective, mentally retarded, or just downright crooked. More than one had departed in haste, two jumps ahead of an enraged populace, never to return.

Sox O'Brien was not of this tribe. Win or lose, he was never afraid to come back. When he skated out that night to handle his third Gold Cup Game he was greeted with groans of derision, which he ignored. He was used to it. Fans always boo the referee. Sox O'Brien realized that it meant nothing personal, that it was merely a sturdy expression of irreverence for authority. The democratic touch.

A stocky, bowlegged man with an underslung jaw, Sox O'Brien refereed hockey games out of sheer zest for combat. Much of his fame derived from a legend that he had once battled his way through an aggrieved crowd in Sudbury armed only with his skates, with which he threatened to chop off the head of any hostile fan who dared lay a finger on him.

From that day his authority was assured. Admirers and detractors alike agreed that whatever his failings, at least Sox O'Brien had guts. Maybe his eyesight wasn't what it used to be. Perhaps he did get a little winded along about the end of the second period. But he had guts. A referee could ask no higher tribute.

Up in the stands, McGonigle glumly watched as the players, with one notable exception, batted the puck around and limbered up their aging joints. That exception was the Snowshoe Lake goalie. The cage stood ominously empty. Around McGonigle, rumours buzzed like bees.

A whisper that the Sieve would appear as usual left gloom in its wake among the hometowners. Someone muttered that if that disaster materialized, the Old-timers Game might as well be abolished forever.

As for the delegates from up the valley, they waited with mixed feelings. They had heard that Unbeatable Bates was actually in town and would definitely appear in the Snowshoe Lake goal. This intelligence was enough to shake anyone. It had, in fact, shaken Caspar Yollik so severely that he was unable to eat his dinner. On the other hand, they had also heard about the Sieve, and prayed earnestly that rumour would manifest itself as a happy fact.

McGonigle sized up the players. For ancients of thirty-five years and more they were sprightly beyond belief.

He had expected a spavined bunch with balding pates and saggy bellies — a creaking crew of erstwhile athletes gone to seed. Bald heads were certainly in evidence, and there was no denying that some of the oldsters were a little broad in the beam; but on the whole they seemed in an excellent state of preservation. A couple of rugged old gentlemen (he judged them to be well out of their thirties) were cavorting at mid-ice with all the abandon of young lambs in springtime. McGonigle, who had assumed that the Old-timer's Game would be a sad spectacle of muscle-bound middle age in slow motion, began to revise his opinions.

"Surprised you, huh?" said Slewfoot.

"They're in better shape than I thought they'd be," McGonigle admitted.

"They take this game serious. Every one of them goes on the wagon a month before the game. They practise every night. And don't forget most of these guys are hardrock miners.

You take a fellow spends eight hours a day underground with a pick and shovel or running a compressed-air drill, he's in pretty fair shape to start with."

McGonigle eyed the empty cage and wondered what was going on in the Snowshoe Lake dressing room. No matter what happened he knew the name of the loser — McGonigle.

If Unbeatable Bates failed to appear the blame would rest on one man, the man who had removed the goalie from the bus — McGonigle.

If the Unbeatable did appear and went down to glassy-eyed defeat, the blame would rest squarely on the shoulders of the idiot who had left the Unbeatable alone and unguarded for an hour with a jug of Slewfoot Special. The name of that idiot — McGonigle.

And if the Unbeatable did appear and by some miracle lived up to his name, to whom would the credit belong, and who would earn the everlasting gratitude of every man, woman, and child in Snowshoe Lake?

"Snead, that's who," muttered McGonigle.

"What say?" asked Mrs. Dinwoodie.

"Talking to myself."

"Don't blame you. If I was in the spot you're in I'd be talking to myself too."

"I don't like the look of that empty net," said Slewfoot.

"He'll show."

"Maybe he got a whiff of that rubbing alcohol they use in the dressing room and passed right out again."

"He'll show," McGonigle repeated stubbornly. "He'll probably fan on every shot, but he'll show. You couldn't keep him out of that cage with a shotgun."

The gate at the end of the arena swung open.

Gloved and padded, brandishing the big flat goalie stick, Unbeatable Bates waddled into view.

Snowshoe Lake welcomed him with a mighty roar of relief. As for the visiting fans they affected a vast nonchalance, as if all goalies were alike to them, but anyone could see that they were shaken to the depths. They stared grimly and in silence, with the exception of Caspar Yollik, who yipped, "Double cross! Somebody double-crossed me."

Unbeatable Bates skated once around the goal, tested the sturdiness of the posts, crouched in the crease, and waited for a warm-up shot. One of the Snowshoe Lake players came in from the blue line and drilled a low shot from fifteen feet out. The puck bounced off the pads.

Slewfoot dug an elbow into McGonigle's ribs.

"B'gosh he's going to be all right. He stopped it."

"A little boy with a ping-pong bat could have stopped it," said McGonigle, unconvinced.

It was after eight-thirty. The crowd, impatient for action, stamped rhythmically. Down at the bench Bobo was arguing with Sox O'Brien. McGonigle could guess why. Bobo was pleading for more warm-up time. The Unbeatable had gone in cold; he needed all the time he could get. And Sox O'Brien was saying, "That's none of my concern. You should have had him dressed sooner." Meanwhile, the Snowshoe Lake players were belting pucks goalward as rapidly as they could. One trouble was that a good many of their shots were away off target. The other was that the on-target shots were getting past Unbeatable Bates. The longer he warmed up the worse he got.

"You're right," said Emma Dinwoodie after a while. "We need a little boy with a ping-pong bat."

McGonigle viewed the spectacle with dismay. The Unbeatable, already drenched with sweat, might snap out of it in time, but his reflexes were off and he was pressing too hard.

"How come he got that nickname?" Slewfoot wanted to know.

Sox O'Brien looked up at the clock. The stamping had become thunderous.

O'Brien blew his whistle. The players lined up. The crowd stood. Musical tributes to Queen and Country droned lugubriously through the amplifier as everyone looked dutifully solemn. An unfortunate scratch on one of the records created the effect of a gargantuan belch over the final notes.

The ritual over, the crowd sent up a cheer of vast relief and sat down. Starting players skated to their positions; the others flocked to their respective benches. Sox O'Brien put his hands on his hips and calmly surveyed the crowd, as if daring anyone to start something. Satisfied that his authority was undisputed, for the moment at least, he wheeled briskly to mid-ice, crouched, and dropped the puck.

The Golden Valley centre trapped it, whacked it across to his right wing. The wing sidestepped his check and headed for the blue line. He tried to cut inside the defence, which was a mistake. Left defence reefed him with a mighty bodycheck. He staggered back as if he had run full tilt into a wall, and went into a wild little dance as he tried to stay on his skates and hang onto his stick. The puck bounced on to the blade of the other defenceman's stick. Instead of carrying it out, he tried to flip over to the wing and laid it squarely in front of the incoming Golden Valley centre.

The centre accepted this gift with no more delay than it took to go into a backswing. He cut loose with a slapshot.

Unbeatable Bates lunged forward. He misjudged. The puck whizzed past his shoulder, under the bar, into a top corner, and dropped spinning to the ice behind him.

There was a moment of shocked, incredulous silence. Then the Golden Valley fans leaped to their feet with a wild howl of joy. They hurled programmes into the air. They pounded each other over the shoulders. They yelled and screamed, cutting loose with an uproar that completely drowned the collective groan that went up from the stunned burghers of Snowshoe Lake. The bagpipes squealed over the thud and boom of the big bass drum.

The game had been in progress for exactly nine seconds.

Dejectedly, McGonigle watched Unbeatable Bates reach his stick into the cage for the puck. He tried to comfort himself with the thought that it could have happened to anyone. Slapshots! They ought to be outlawed. The man who fired one never knew where it was going and neither did anyone else.

The Golden Valley band was thumping vigorously away at "There'll Be a Hot Time in the Old Town Tonight," with outlandish discord, when the centres faced off again. The jubilation of the visitors was a long time simmering down. From the depths of shock into which they had been plunged by the appearance of Unbeatable Bates they had soared into heights of wildest optimism. The Unbeatable had been tried and found beatable after all. Even Caspar Yollik was braying as if he had never known a moment of doubt.

Sticks clashed and bodies thudded against the boards as play resumed. The Snowshoe Lake players dug in. There was only one thing to do about a nine-second goal. Get it back and start over. And for the next five minutes they went roaring in over the blue line and swarmed around the Golden Valley net with sticks and elbows high.

Thud! A Valley defenceman tried to belt an incoming forward, missed, and went crashing into the boards. *Clunk!* A Snowshoe Lake shot from the wing hit a goalpost. *Boom!* Another shot bounced off the backboards. It was wild give and take until a desperate defenceman golfed at the puck, and a wing shook himself loose, snared it at centre ice, and streaked away with the whole Snowshoe Lake team in frantic pursuit. He made it across the blue line just as the Snowshoe Lake centre overhauled him.

He barely managed to get the puck away. A weak shot, with little power and scant direction. The puck popped into the air, came down four feet in front of the net and bounced. Normally Unbeatable Bates or any other goalie on earth over the peewee age limit would have gobbled it up.

The puck took another bounce. It cleared his stick and rolled. Horrified, Unbeatable Bates whacked at it with his stick and missed. The puck wobbled wearily across the line and fell flat, just inside the post, as Bates dove for it and missed it with his outstretched glove.

He sprawled there in the red glow of the goal light.

Golden Valley fans became hysterical all over again. As for the hometowners they were dazed. A stupefied silence descended upon them.

"Any goalie who fans on a shot like that," said Emma finally, "couldn't keep a basketball out of a phone booth."

"I guess the lad ain't well," said Slewfoot.

"And no wonder. He's still hung over from that elixir of yours. Probably saw three pucks and swatted the wrong one." Emma watched Sox O'Brien scoop up the puck and return to mid-ice. "It isn't the money," she added. "I've been broke before and I'll be broke again. But I feel like I've been cold-clocked."

McGonigle heaved himself to his feet.

"Be seeing you," he said.

"No point in going out and shootin' yourself," advised Slewfoot. "Nobody blames you. It was my fault."

"Something I've got to do," replied McGonigle. He edged his way past a long row of crestfallen Snowshoe Lakers. He had to find Uncle Wilmer.

22

"They Never Come Back"

It was true, as McGonigle had told Uncle Wilmer, that even the effort of bending over to tie his own shoelaces left him breathless nowadays. In the steamy dressing room, wearing Hardrock Valenti's beat-up outfit, he was puffing when he straightened up, heaved himself off the bench and clumped around to get the feel of the skates. The boots fitted snugly over the heavy uniform socks.

"The boy will give you a stick," Uncle Wilmer said. "They're all out at the bench."

McGonigle picked up Valenti's big gloves and put them on.

"Don't expect anything," he said. "I'm long over the hill, and nobody knows it better."

"I know," said Uncle Wilmer. He extended his hand. "Skates, I want to tell you I appreciate this."

"Like I said, don't expect anything. I can't help your club. Any one of those fellows out there can skate me into the ice."

"Maybe. And could be you might surprise yourself."

McGonigle shook his head. "Ten years too late. You know what they say about fighters. They never come back. Hockey players, too."

"Come along. About five minutes left in the period. I told Bobo."

Uncle Wilmer opened the dressing room door. McGonigle clumped out into the short corridor that ended at the bench. The fans were roaring. A huge shout went up — the unmistakable shout that greets a goal. The Golden Valley band blared and boomed in triumph.

"Sounds like another one," said Uncle Wilmer.

The Golden Valley fans were whooping it up while the home crowd slouched in mute dejection. At the Snowshoe Lake bench Bobo Strowger was sending out a fresh forward line and trying to rally his forces. "Get out there and hit!" he bawled. "Slow 'em up. Step into them, you guys." McGonigle caught a glimpse of the scoreboard with the big three and the round goose egg. The score wasn't as lopsided as he expected. Judging by the Unbeatable's performance in the first few minutes of the game he wouldn't have been surprised if the score had climbed into double figures by now. The Golden Valley band played lustily. The bagpipes squealed.

Snowshoe Lake forwards stumbled though the gate and slumped disconsolately to the bench as the relief line climbed over the fence. Uncle Wilmer tapped Bobo's shoulder. Bobo turned. He stared at McGonigle.

"I don't believe it," he said.

"Nobody's asking you." McGonigle selected a stick. A war club. "I'm in lousy shape, so don't look for any skating. Maybe I can steer them away from Bates."

Bobo waved right defence to the bench.

"More power to you, Skates," he said. "Let's go."

Sox O'Brien was crouched for the face-off as McGonigle skated into position. The ice was strange under him but he was surprised to find that he could stay on his feet. Ten years. He had thought he would probably fall flat on his face. But it was like swimming or riding a bicycle. It always came back to you.

The puck fell. The Golden Valley uproar almost drowned the booming voice over the PA "Subbing for Valenti... Snowshoe Lake...Number 4...McGonigle." A wild cheer went up from a few Snowshoe Lake fans who realized that this was *the* McGonigle, but by and large the announcement didn't register, for which McGonigle was grateful. He saw a Golden Valley forward belting toward him, glanced to his left and found no one in the clear, carefully steered his man into the boards and tied him up. The check retrieved the puck and went scrambling off out over the blue line.

McGonigle followed up, watchfully, ready to move up to the other blue line if an attack developed. It didn't. He dropped back as the Golden Valley centre came roaring down the middle lane, edged over a little. The centre tried to go through. McGonigle dropped him, took the puck, swung around, laid it out to the uncovered wing again.

The puck clicked neatly on the blade of the stick. A good pass. Not too hard; not too soft. The wing wheeled and broke away. He got past the red line before he was checked but whacked the puck into the corner. McGonigle moved up slowly. *Wham!* Two men smashed into the backboards, and a Golden Valley player fanned on the loose puck. A scramble, with everyone surging around the goal. The puck skimmed out to the point. McGonigle had to reach for it, but he stopped it before it went over the blue line. Out of the corner of his eye he saw a Snowshoe Lake player shake loose; he laid down the pass. Again, it was right on the stick blade. A screened shot, with the Golden Valley defence trying to come out. He had a glimpse of the goalie sliding across the crease with a big glove lunging. The red light flashed. Sox O'Brien's whistle shrilled.

Snowshoe Lake went crazy. They sprang to their feet, with arms outstretched, howling hosannas like instant converts at a revival meeting. They had been waiting hopelessly for this through fifteen minutes of unmitigated gloom. They bounced into stark delirium.

Up on the scoreboard the goose egg vanished in favour of a bold and upright 1.

McGonigle waited in a half-crouch, his stick across his knees, economizing his strength. He would need every moment of rest he could get. He called on the memories of his final year in the big league when he knew the legs were gone. Boxcar Moodie was coaching then, and Boxcar had lasted a long time.

"Make every move count," Boxcar said. "Don't take a step that doesn't mean something. Block off the angles; steer 'em into the corners; tie 'em up. As for the big wind-up around the net and the rush down the middle, forget it. That used to bring the crowd up screamin' when you were a young fella, but how many goals did it get you? Do that now, and it'll leave you pooped. The forwards will be sailin' by you so fast you'll catch cold in the draft. Take your time, set up your plays, make 'em come to you, and save your strength."

Rocking-chair hockey, but it had given him an extra season. Ten years ago. Now he'd be lucky if it gave him an extra twenty minutes.

Faceoff, with the home crowd still roaring. A Snowshoe Lake player got jammed against the boards, and the puck came skittering out across the blue line with a Golden Valley man legging it in pursuit as his line mates shook themselves clear to back up the play. McGonigle carried the puck behind the net and waited, calmly sizing up the situation. A couple of reckless old-timers came charging in on him. Sucker play. He flipped the puck out to the uncovered wing just as the enemy hit him.

Crunch! They were slow, but even at that they nailed him. They rocked him. He was belted into the boards, knocked off balance, and the ice came up to hit him. But he brought one of the attackers down with him and trapped the man's stick under his elbow. He could see the play moving off down the ice as his opponent stumbled to his feet, wrenching the stick free. Every second you could keep a man immobilized was a second gained.

But McGonigle was grunting as he got back on his skates. A few smashes like that would take a lot out of a man. Ten years ago he would have faded away from them, leaving the enemy chewing splinters. But this was now. He couldn't even sidestep an old-timer.

Unbeatable Bates was looking anxiously at him over the crossbar.

"You okay?"

McGonigle grinned at him. "Never felt a thing." But he was breathing heavily as he skated up the ice. There was a great scramble going on around the other cage. And then the siren wailed, Sox O'Brien blew his whistle and scooped up the puck. The period was over. McGonigle swung over to the gate and joined the players clumping to the dressing room.

He found a bench and sat down. He was surprised to find that he was wet with perspiration. It streamed down his forehead and into his eyes, and dripped from his chin. Someone handed him a towel. He mopped his face and the back of his neck. Unbeatable Bates sat down beside him.

"I wish I was dead," muttered the goalie. "Thought that period would never end. I blew three."

"Forget it."

"Three soft, lousy shots! A baby could have picked them off. Three stinking easy ones."

"We'll get 'em back," said McGonigle. "How do you feel?"

"Better than when I went out there. First five minutes I was seein' two pucks. Man, was I terrible!"

"It's behind you now," said McGonigle. "Saw a goalie beat for five one night. All in the first period. But he went on to win."

"With another goalie."

McGonigle shook his head. "Same guy. It wasn't all his fault. He didn't have much protection. But we pulled up our socks and got him a couple. He played shut-out hockey the rest of the way."

There was little talk in the dressing room. Most of the old-timers were resigned. And a two-goal deficit, with an unsteady man in the net, doesn't inspire jolly conversation. Tactfully, they left Unbeatable Bates severely alone. After all, what do you say to a hotshot goalie who has just fanned on three soft ones? You can't pretend it didn't happen. And you don't kid him about it either. You leave him to his thoughts.

Bobo Strowger bustled in.

"Men," he said, "you got a bad period out of your system. They're beginning to fade. I can see it. We're coming on and they're on the run. And we've got a big man going for us now. Skates McGonigle. You saw how he stiffened up that defence. Skates, we're obliged to you for helping out."

"Do the best I can," mumbled McGonigle. "Not in shape, but I'll give it a try."

"Good man." Bobo slapped him on the shoulder. He hovered over Unbeatable Bates. "How you feeling now, boy?"

"I'd hate to tell you," said the Unbeatable. "But they're not going to get any more, I'll promise you that." He looked down the dressing room. "You guys get those two goals back, and we're in."

The old-timers listened respectfully but without noticeable enthusiasm. They were realists. If Golden Valley could get three they would probably add a few more. Unbeatable Bates had turned out to be just another big name with an overblown reputation. As for McGonigle, who he? Another big name, but from an era that antedated even the old-timers. Most likely he wouldn't last half way through the next period.

The same thought was in McGonigle's mind. He had survived five minutes. But how about forty? Or even twenty? Rough times lay ahead.

When they trooped out again Bobo waved him to the bench.

"Take it easy," said Bobo.

But Golden Valley came roaring in right from the faceoff and pushed the defence around. They stormed around the Snowshoe Lake goal and got in close for a couple of blistering shots. The Unbeatable was a little steadier now, and he blocked both the tries, although he was clearly unsteady on one and lucky on the other. But he made the stops somehow, which gave cheer to the home crowd. Just the same, the attack went on. Golden Valley gave the defence a hard time. The Unbeatable was getting scant protection. A forward got in for a sizzling drive that barely skimmed over the crossbar. There was a scramble, with Bates diving headlong to nail a loose puck just outside the crease, a fraction of a second before a stick whacked at it. Four players sprawled in the pile-up.

"Better get out there," Bobo told McGonigle when Sox O'Brien's whistle halted the play.

McGonigle went out again. Play it cosy; break up the attacks with a minimum of exertion; give the Unbeatable some protection; watch for the chance to shake a man loose with a long pass. But the puck hadn't been dropped fifteen seconds before a Snowshoe Lake forward reefed an opponent into the boards. Penalty.

With the man advantage the enemy put on the power play. The puck flew from stick to stick, off the net, and into the backboards and out again. The Unbeatable crouching, bobbing and weaving, alert for the screened shots. McGonigle caught a man coming in with his head down and clobbered him. He steered another into a corner, chased him behind the net, took the puck away, and took his time. He looked for the opening and scooped the puck down the ice. They roared right back at him. This was when you had to work. By the time the penalty was up and the teams were at even strength, McGonigle was gasping. Bobo called him in. He fell through the gate and sank to the bench, his lungs on fire, his eyes blinded with sweat.

The next goal came like a jolt of lightning. Half way through the period, after the game had settled down to an even pattern of attack and counterattack, it came from a routine faceoff inside the Valley blue line. The Valley centre won the draw, juggled the puck for a moment, and tried to flip it over to a wing. He flubbed it. The puck took a crazy bounce. A wheeling Snowshoe Lake forward caught a glimpse of it and took a backhanded swing. It caught the goalie flatfooted. The puck whipped into the rigging before he could move.

McGonigle, back on the ice by now, felt a stir of hope. He was getting tired; the stick and the skates had become heavy. But the old-timers were beginning to slow down. For all that they were strong men and in good shape, they too had passed the age when muscles seem made of tough elastic. If he could give the Unbeatable enough protection to get into the final period no worse than a goal down there might be a chance.

Golden Valley made a line change, and the fresh men were sore about that lucky goal. They stormed across the blue line. Skating backward, McGonigle tried to steer the puck carrier into the corner, but the man cut sharply inside. McGonigle couldn't get a piece of him.

He saw the Unbeatable lunging out to take the puck on his chest protector. The puck bounced. McGonigle went after the rebound just as a green sweater loomed up in front of him. He was a little off balance when the green shirt slammed into him and sent him down. He crashed against the post before he hit the ice with a thud that knocked the wind out of him.

Everyone was in on the scramble. Someone sprawled over him. There was a wild surge of skates, sticks, uniforms, and plunging bodies. He could see the puck lying in the clear, just off the far post. The Unbeatable was down now, flopping and flailing. McGonigle got to his knees. He saw the flat goalie stick reach out and miss the puck by an inch. Another stick came from nowhere and lifted the puck over the Unbeatable, whipped it into the cage.

There was a red glow. Sox O'Brien's whistle was shrilling. The sound cut through the frenzied roar of the Golden Valley fans. McGonigle seized the goalpost for support and slowly hauled himself to his feet. He felt a twinge of pain in his left knee.

The players sorted themselves out. The Unbeatable whacked at the puck in disgust and banged it out to Sox O'Brien. Up on the scoreboard a 3 became a 4, above the 2.

And that was the way it was when the period ended, and McGonigle clumped slowly back to the dressing room on skates like lead.

23

The Long Twenty Minutes

Slewfoot heard a sniffle. He glanced at Emma and caught her dabbing her eyes with a handkerchief.

"Oh now, wait a minute," he said. "No point carryin' on like that."

"Shut up," she said in a muffled voice.

"I admit it don't look good but nobody *cries* over a hockey game."

"Who's crying? I got a cold in my head." She sniffled again and put the handkerchief away. "The poor guy. He's trying so hard, and he's all tuckered out. Did you see him come off the ice? Could hardly lift one foot after the other."

"He's bushed, that's for sure. Sweat pourin' off him like he fell in a rain barrel."

"The poor guy," she repeated.

Three rows away, Susie looked up at the solemn face of Tim Beckett. She squeezed his hand.

"Don't take it so hard. They've still got another period to play."

"He can still play defence," marvelled Tim. "Plays it like an old pro. He's forgotten more about it than most of those fellows ever knew. But the legs are gone. He's through for the night."

To Tim, who could play all day without a moment of weariness, it was hard to imagine that a time could ever come when the muscles wouldn't respond, when the legs wouldn't do what you asked of them, when exhaustion could drag you down. But it happened. It happened to them all. Some soon, some late. He wished he could go down to the bench when the period began and say, "Sit it out, Skates. You've earned a rest. I'll take over for you." He wouldn't have the experience, all the knowledge Skates McGonigle had acquired over the years, but at least he'd have the strength and speed McGonigle had lost. He'd still be in there at the finish.

Down in the dressing room McGonigle lay on the rubbing table. The trainer's fingers kneaded aching muscles but the aches didn't diminish. The knee was taped now. He felt a dull jab of pain every time he moved it. And his lungs were burning.

Bobo looked down at him.

"Skates," he said, "no matter how it turns out, you've done a great job for us. And I want you to know I appreciate it."

"We all appreciate it," said one of the old-timers. "It's an honour to have you with us."

"Let's get some goals," McGonigle said. "We've got 'em on the run."

Sox O'Brien put his head in the door.

"Let's go," he shouted.

They trooped out silently. McGonigle tried to keep his shoulders up, fought against favouring the knee. But he felt eighty years old. And the knee wasn't right.

"Look," said Bobo to his players. "They're just as tired as you are. Hit 'em. They'll make mistakes. Just get me those two goals back."

He sent McGonigle out on the starting line-up. It was true, as Bobo said, that Golden Valley was tiring. Right from the faceoff it was clear that they had been told to play defensive hockey. Protect that two-goal lead. Let Snowshoe Lake carry the play. Wait for the breaks. And in the first few minutes the break came on a long, long pass that sent a Golden Valley forward into the clear with open ice all the way to the goal. McGonigle tried to catch him but the puck carrier out-footed him and cruised in. Unbeatable Bates crouched, waiting. The crowd screeched. The forward tried to deke the Unbeatable.

Better men had tried it. Once he made his move, he knew he had made a mistake. The Unbeatable had given him an opening and then moved swiftly to cover it. Bates took the puck on his glove and batted it away. McGonigle, coming in, picked it up, and swung round. He sucked in great gasps of air as he skated laboriously across the blue line, up the middle lane, looking for a receiver. There wasn't a man uncovered. He could hear the scrape of skates on ice as the man behind him closed the gap.

McGonigle drew back his stick and let go. He felt the solid impact of wood against rubber. The puck sailed. He saw a green-sweatered arm flash out and miss. He saw the green-sweatered goalie lunge across the net. He didn't see the puck go in, because by then he was being shouldered and spun around. He staggered and sprawled to the ice. But the great roar that went up and the blink of the red goal light told him all he needed to know.

Exhausted, he got to his knees. The roof echoed to the wild rejoicing of the home crowd as his mates surged around him and hauled him to his feet, pounded him on the back, and rubbed the top of his balding head. He limped to the bench. Bobo was screaming, as the relief forwards tumbled over the boards.

"Pour it on! Don't let 'em get set. Dump it in and go after it."

Both elbows on the rail, McGonigle fought for air as he watched the blurred figures on the ice. He was drained of strength. His head was numb. He ached from his neck to his heels. And when a Snowshoe Lake forward was dumped headlong at the ten-minute mark and Sox O'Brien thumbed a Valley defenceman, McGonigle could feel only a sluggish resentment. It was a break, it gave the home team an edge, but it meant he had to go back to the ice. Any penalty meant work for the defence.

A penalty against you meant double duty breaking up the enemy attack; a penalty against the other team meant that you had to play up, guarding against a breakaway, and it meant that the enemy would fire the puck the length of the ice whenever they could, and that you had to recover it, lug it back, try to set up a play. You could skate miles. And just then McGonigle doubted if he could skate the width of the rink without collapsing.

Bobo sent him out. As he expected, Golden Valley scooped the puck into the farthest corner. He slogged after it, carried it behind the net, moved up slowly, laid down the pass as soon as he reached the blue line and followed it in, waiting at the point as Snowshoe Lake worked inside on the power play. They bungled it. The puck came soaring down the ice again.

Panting, McGonigle went back. But this time the clearing shot was on the net and the Unbeatable saved him a few steps, flipped the puck up to him. McGonigle wheeled slowly and passed it up to centre, and again moved up to the point. He was just in time to trap the puck as a Valley forward broke up the attack and bounced the puck off the boards. McGonigle banged it the width of the ice to a mate who had shaken loose.

This time the power play clicked. A long low shot that was kicked out, another shot, a rebound, a goalie flopping in the crease, a deflected shot and on went the light. The score was tied.

Snowshoe Lake went into a noisy state of complete lunacy. As for McGonigle he experienced nothing more than a sense of relief. Without even waiting to catch Bobo's eye he dragged himself over to the gate, stumbled in, and collapsed on the bench. The trainer draped a towel over the back of his neck.

His heart was pounding; he was saturated with sweat and so utterly exhausted that he had no further interest in what happened on the ice. The players surged back and forth, sticks clashed, the puck bounced off the boards, men chased each other into the corners, collided and fell. It was just a lot of meaningless movement. All he wanted to do was crawl into the dressing room and die quietly.

The roaring of the crowd came up in great waves and subsided and welled up again. Both teams were dog-tired. Players weren't carrying the puck any more; they were getting rid of it. The Old-timers' Game wasn't a hockey game any more; it was a fiendish test of endurance. And as the minutes went by the two figures on the scoreboard, the 4 above and the 4 below testified to the deadlock.

Eight minutes left. Six. Five. Four. Snowshoe Lake drew a penalty, and the Valley team sent out five forwards. But the Unbeatable was a well man again, living up to his name. They had five shots on him in those two minutes, and he kicked out two of them, batted two into the corners with his big glove, and smothered the other in a pileup at the crease. A Snowshoe Lake defenceman was helped off the ice, one leg dragging. McGonigle felt Bobo's hand on his shoulder.

"Can you make it, Skates?"

He pushed himself up from the rail, gripped the gate for a moment, and stumbled out. When his skates touched the ice he almost fell. He skated over to his position. You didn't tell a manager to send out someone else, that you didn't have an ounce of strength left. You went out and did what you could.

The faceoff was in the circle to the left of the net. The puck dropped. The Valley centre whacked it across to a wing. A shot skimmed past the post, rattled off the backboards and came out the far side. McGonigle picked it up and lumbered down the ice. He saw a greenshirt coming at him, and he shifted. The greenshirt smashed into the boards and went down. McGonigle stumbled across the blue line. He heard a shout, saw one of his own men in the clear, away over on the other side of the rink.

He laid down the pass and had the good feeling that it was dead on, neither so far ahead that it would beat the receiver across the enemy blue line, nor so far behind that he would have to swing back to pick it up. But he didn't see what happened to it, because he was belted by a greenshirt half a second after the puck left his stick. He hit the ice sprawling. And as he lay there on the cold surface, trying to summon strength enough to crawl to his feet the rink seemed to explode with sound. A long distance off he could see a red light shining and players were swarming around the man who had fired the puck home, as the Snowshoe Lake crowd went out of its collective mind.

24

Business Methods in Snowshoe Lake

There hadn't been a celebration like it in Snowshoe Lake since the night the liquor store burned down. Caspar Yollik and a couple of fellow sportsmen from Golden Valley collared Sox O'Brien after the game and made anguished noises about the unfairness of it all, but the referee advised them, unkindly they thought, to drop dead.

"Exhibition game," snapped O'Brien. "No residence rules that I know of. And anyway you had a couple of ringers on your own club, under phony names. You want to go into that?"

The Golden Valley management decided that they didn't care to go into that little matter, and Mr. Yollik was advised to shut up and pay up. Later, over in the Lakeshore, his grief was so tumultuous when Al, the stakeholder, was paying off that a few citizens wondered aloud if Mr. Yollik might be cooled off by an escorted tour of Snowshoe Lake in his underwear. Nothing further was heard from Mr. Yollik.

The only Golden Valley supporter who presented himself at the pay-off desk was old Mr. Wildgoose. He was roundly condemned for lack of faith and secretly envied for uncommonly shrewd judgement, but he merely said that he never let patriotism shake him loose from a hunch; some inner voice had told him that Snowshoe Lake was about due.

A few dejected losers noted that the Wildgoose's hunches had been paying him dividends for a long time; there was a legend that Mr. Wildgoose had once rescued an Indian youngster from drowning and that the lad's grandmother had given him a specially treated rabbit's foot by way of reward. The legend now became more firmly established than ever, and when Mr. Wildgoose was questioned about it he merely smiled a mysterious smile and said that rabbits' feet were only lucky for fast rabbits.

In the old-timers' dressing room, where the old-timers broke training with the aid of half a dozen cases of beer supplied by a grateful management, the racket was deafening. It subsided merely a little when Blackjack Snead pushed his way into the room, all smiles and handshakes.

"Didn't I tell you I'd get you a goalie?" he reminded them, as he slapped the Unbeatable on the shoulder. "Charlie, you were terrific. Wasn't he terrific, fellows?"

"I was lousy," said the Unbeatable. He flicked a thumb toward McGonigle. "Thank him."

"Skates," said Blackjack Snead, handsomely, "we've had our little differences in the past, all in the line of business, but I've always admired you. One of the great players in the game. But I never admired you as much as I did tonight. You played big. Real big. And it was big of you to play."

The exhausted McGonigle, aching in every muscle, looked up from the rubbing table.

"Blackjack," he said, "I did it all for you."

The office door opened. Bobo looked out.

"Blackjack," he shouted. "Will you come in for a minute?"

Snead moved toward the door. He turned for a last word.

"And this is only the beginning," he said. "You've won the Old-timers' Game. I'm glad I was able to help. But just watch your junior team this winter. They're going to win everything in sight. And next year. And the year after. My club is going to put Snowshoe Lake on the map."

There were no cries of gratitude as he vanished into the office.

"What does he mean, put us on the map?" muttered the man who had scored the winning goal. "We've been on the map ever since they dug the shaft for the Snowshoe Mine."

In the office Blackjack Snead found that Bobo had company.

"Tim, boy," beamed Blackjack, hand extended. "Wasn't that some game?"

"Tim has something to say to you, Blackjack." Bobo seemed apprehensive.

"Well, I've got a lot to say to Tim. We've got great plans for you, lad. I was on the phone to the office tonight, just before the game. Yes sir, great plans…"

"You can't have any plans for me, Mr. Snead. I'm not playing for you."

Blackjack Snead's eyes narrowed a little but there was no fading of his smile.

"Tim," he said easily, "maybe Bobo hasn't explained the situation to you. Perhaps you're not happy about this sponsorship deal but the whole point is that you can't do anything about it. This is your club, boy, and you just can't play for anyone else."

"Then I'd rather not play at all, Mr. Snead."

"Oh come on now, lad. You know you can't give up hockey."

"I don't want to give it up. But Mr. McGonigle lost his job on my account. If I can't play for him, I won't play for anyone."

"Who put you up to this?" inquired Snead.

"No one. After seeing what Mr. McGonigle did tonight, I knew what I wanted to do. I've told Uncle Wilmer. He says he's going to talk to you."

Tim opened the door to the dressing room.

"Now wait a minute. Wait a minute. You can't do this. We signed an agreement with your hockey club. You can't let them down."

"No use arguing, Mr. Snead. I won't play for you."

"Then you won't play at all. Think it over, boy."

"I could always go and play for Tomcat Creek. I'd hate to do that. I don't think folks around here would like it very much."

"Tim!" yelled Bobo. "You wouldn't."

"I'd have to, Bobo. It's a free country. Nobody owns me. Excuse me. I want to talk to Mr. McGonigle."

He went out to the dressing room. Snead stared at Bobo.

"What's going on? What's he trying to pull?"

"He means it, Blackjack. And he'll make it stick. What good is your agreement if the boy doesn't go along? All you'll have is a small-town hockey club without a star." Bobo was sweating. "Blackjack, don't you realize what happened tonight? McGonigle is a ruddy hero."

"I don't care how much of a hero he is. We still own your hockey club."

"Blackjack, use your head. After what he did out there tonight McGonigle can have anything he wants in this town."

"Then you'll have to tell them different."

"If they want to break the agreement I can't help you. I've got my own future to think of."

"*Your* future!" exploded Snead. "I'll fix your future. We'll find someone else to run the club."

"You'd have to. I wouldn't have a friend in town. I'd get along," said Bobo. "Tomcat Creek made me an offer last month to move up there and run their rink. Like Tim, I'd hate to do it but if he was on my club maybe we'd make out all right."

Out in the dressing room Tim went over to the rubbing table.

"How are you feeling, Skates?"

McGonigle looked up at him and grinned painfully. Even the muscles of his face were aching.

"Terrible," he grunted. "But inside I feel pretty good."

"You might have killed yourself."

"Can you think of a better way to go?"

"Skates, would it help get your job back if I promised to sign with the Blueshirts? If you ever want me?"

"Sign a C-form? Your parents would have to okay it."

"I'll talk to them. I know what I want to do, Skates. After what you said yesterday — if I have something I want to use it. If I'm good enough to make the big league, that's where I want to be. And I won't sign with anyone but you. Would it help?"

"Why sure," grinned McGonigle. "I think it would help quite a lot."

Blackjack Snead had just left Bobo's office, muttering about the ingratitude of mankind, when he ran into Uncle Wilmer hotfooting it down the corridor with Emma Dinwoodie and Slewfoot. They had come from an agreeable session with Caspar Yollik at the Lakeshore.

"Just the man we're looking for!" bellowed Uncle Wilmer. From his inner pocket he fished out the hockey club's copy of the agreement. "See this, Mr. Snead?"

"I see it. And I'm holding you to it, Mr. Kirby."

"You're not holding me to anything," said Uncle Wilmer. He ripped the document in half, from top to bottom. "The whole executive just resigned, including me. Meet the new president."

"Hi," said Slewfoot.

"And the new vice-president."

"Hi," said Emma.

"And as new president," said Slewfoot, "I want to say that any agreements signed by the old executive don't count no more."

"That's what you think," replied Snead.

"As for you, Mr. Snead, I got three words to say. Who needs you?" Out of Slewfoot's pocket came a huge fistful of bills, which he flourished under Snead's nose. "The hockey club is no longer broke, on account I am making a donation to the treasury."

"Likewise," added Emma, opening her purse.

"All I can say," observed Blackjack Snead with considerable bitterness, "is that this is one hell of a way to do business."

"Maybe so. But it's the way we do business in Snowshoe Lake," Uncle Wilmer informed him.

25

McGonigle's Farewell

In the Blueshirts' head office a little after ten o'clock the next morning, Ben Dooley accepted the collect call for the sheer pleasure of telling McGonigle that he was still fired. But McGonigle didn't give him a chance.

"And you say the club tore up an agreement with Blackjack Snead, because the boy wouldn't go along with it? Because he won't sign with anyone but *you*?"

"That's right."

"And you say the boy is good?"

"For his age, Ben, he's the best I've ever seen."

"Wonderful. You've signed him up, of course."

"No, Ben. I haven't."

"Why not?"

"Ben, the boy trusts me. He'll sign anything I ask him. So will his mother. I could tie him up so tightly he wouldn't be able to do a thing for the rest of his hockey life without our say-so."

"So what? That's the idea," shouted Dooley. "That's why you're there."

"Ben, it's a free country. As I said, the boy trusts me. This deal, I just want it to be a handshake. I don't want to tie him down to anything until he's ready to sign a proper contract of his own free will and knowing what he's doing."

"What's the matter with you, Skates? Have you gone and got religion or something? Are you out of your head? You've conned dozens of kids and their parents into signing C-forms. That's your job. You fool around like this, and we could lose that boy. Snap out of it!"

"You won't lose him. Put him on your negotiation list for protection if you like, but if he and I shake hands on it he'll keep his promise. And that's the way I want it to be, Ben."

"I never heard you talk so foolish. That northern air must have gone to your skull. You trim Blackjack Snead out of an ironclad agreement and now you're talking about handshake deals. We can *do* things for this kid."

"I know we can. But I want it to be his own choice. Like I said, Ben, it's a free country. And look, Ben."

"I'm looking."

"You fired me yesterday."

"Oh come off it, Skates. You know how it was. Maybe I was a little hasty, but..."

"Didn't you mean it?"

"Of course I meant it. But now that you've outsmarted Snead, it's different."

"Ben, if you won't go for a handshake deal with the boy, I guess I'll just have to stay fired."

Ben Dooley sighed.

"It's your deal. Your handshake. Go ahead. Come back to work."

"I'll fly back this afternoon."

"Skates — tell me one thing. How did you swing it?"

"I played hockey for Snowshoe Lake last night. Big game of the year. Real rugged stuff. We won."

"You played *what* last night?"

"Hockey. The folks up here are kind of grateful to me for helping them out. I've got to go now, Ben. Bye now."

Ben Dooley put down the phone. "Says he played hockey last night," he told Ginger. "I don't believe it."

"Neither do I," said Miss Gillespie.

"It would have killed him."

"In the shape he's in, that's for sure. Who does he think he's kidding?" She went back to her work, snickering.

McGonigle emerged from the phone booth in the Lakeshore lobby. Uncle Wilmer was waiting for him, with Bobo Strowger and Slewfoot.

"Have we got a new sponsor?" Bobo asked.

"You can have one if you want," McGonigle said, "but with all the money the club has in the treasury this morning, who needs it?" He turned to Uncle Wilmer. "Would you rather run your own store or be a branch of a hardware chain run from Toronto?"

"That's a dopey question," said Uncle Wilmer. "More fun running my own store."

"In a few years," McGonigle told them, "you'll almost have to have a big-league hook-up to survive. Hockey's moving that way. But why not run your own club as long as you can? Stay free. It's more fun."

McGonigle looked around the lobby.

"The airport bus will be here any minute," he said. "Where's Emma?"

The street door opened. Tim Beckett came in with his mother and Susie. Mrs. Beckett walked over to McGonigle.

"I said that if anyone tried to talk my boy into signing anything I'd take Tim right off the team," she told him.

"I haven't asked anyone to sign anything, Mrs. Beckett."

"Tim seems to have made up his mind he wants to play for you, Mr. McGonigle. I guess there's no use trying to talk him out of it. He said something about a paper called a C-form."

"No need, Mrs. Beckett. Tim and I don't need any more than a handshake. Right, Tim?"

Tim shook hands. "If you say so, Mr. McGonigle."

Mrs. Beckett was puzzled.

"And you don't want me to sign any paper?"

"Wait until your husband comes home," he said. "Wait until you have all talked it over. When you're sure of what Tim wants and what you want for him, if it's hockey we'll be glad to have him."

"This year?" Susie was anxious.

McGonigle shook his head. "He's got to stay at school. And Snowshoe Lake has to win the championship. Isn't this to be The Year?"

"This," said Bobo, "is definitely going to be The Year."

Susie flung her arms around McGonigle's neck and kissed him.

"What's that for?" he asked her.

"That's for helping him. And for leaving him with us a while longer."

Through the big front window McGonigle could see the bus lumbering down the snowy street. He went upstairs. The door of Emma Dinwoodie's room was open. She was packing a suitcase.

"You leaving?" he asked. "On this bus?"

She shook her head, without turning around.

"Not right away," she said in a muffled voice. "Another bus. This afternoon."

"Where do you go?"

"Back home. To Haileybury." She pulled a strap tight and buckled it.

"Will there be someone there to meet you?"

Emma turned around. She looked very small and forlorn, and when McGonigle saw her clear blue eyes he had a notion that she had been crying.

"No," she said. "I live alone in my own house. I'm used to it." She held out her hand. "Skates McGonigle, I'm glad we met up. It's been nice knowing you. Have a good trip back."

The firm, cool hand. The clear eyes. The warm smile. McGonigle felt a sudden unfamiliar sadness and sense of loss. He was going to miss Emma Dinwoodie.

"Goodbye, Skates."

Her voice was steady enough, but it betrayed her. McGonigle put his arms around her. She buried her face against his overcoat. He could feel the beating of her heart. She was shaking.

"I'm going to miss you so awfully much," she said in a smothered voice. Her fingers dug into his sleeves.

"Look," said McGonigle, unsteadily. "I'm going to miss you too. But there's no sense to that. Why should we have to? Miss each other, I mean." He was speaking over the top of her head to the frosty window pane. "I've just come to realize I've got mighty fond of you, Emma."

Down below, the airport bus ground to a stop and honked peevishly.

"Dooley says I always gum things up. It's the only thing he can depend on, he says. That I'll gum things up. But look...I don't want to say goodbye to you."

The bus honked again. She looked up at him. He kissed her. The experience was so pleasant that he kissed her again, with great vigour and enthusiasm.

"Holy smoke!" said McGonigle in an astonished voice. "I've gone and fallen in love with you. That's what it is. I'm in love with you, Emma."

"Excuse me," rasped a familiar voice. "I hate to interrupt, McGonigle, but if you're taking this bus you'd better get a move on."

Blackjack Snead, suitcase in hand, stood in the open doorway. McGonigle was in such a state that it didn't even occur to him to advise Snead to drop dead. Instead, he beamed in a silly sort of way and merely said. "Be right with you, Blackjack."

Snead went on downstairs. Emma put her arms around McGonigle's neck and drew his head down. She kissed him again.

"You've got to leave," she said, and pushed him toward the door.

"Give me that suitcase," he said. "You're coming with me."

Emma shook her head. "It's a nice thought," she admitted, "but I must go home."

"Hold everything," said McGonigle. "I can't let you go now."

"Ben Dooley is expecting you. If you don't show up, he'll think you're back to your old ways again."

"But wait a minute! When are we going to see each other again?"

"Whenever you like. I could come down to the city the day after tomorrow."

"Is that a promise?"

"We could take in a hockey game or something."

"Or something," agreed McGonigle. "Like getting married, for instance."

"Do you mean it, Skates?"

"Would you have me?"

"It's a date," said Emma Dinwoodie.

They hurried downstairs. In the lobby he kissed her again, to the unbounded astonishment of all beholders, not because of the kiss but because of the extraordinary enthusiasm he put into it, and climbed on the bus, promising to phone her from Toronto that night. McGonigle sat down by a window. Uncle Wilmer, Slewfoot, Tim, Mrs. Beckett, and Susie were all waving to him and shouting goodbye. He waved back. Pink-faced, Emma Dinwoodie called out, "I'll be waiting."

The bus lurched into motion. Blackjack Snead sat down beside him.

"Nice people," said Snead.

"The best," replied McGonigle, all in a glow.

"No hard feelings?" inquired Blackjack.

McGonigle shrugged.

"Nope," he said. "All in the game."

"I had to give it a try," said Blackjack. "After all, the Beckett kid *is* a natural. We both know that."

The bus rolled down Main Street.

"Nice woman, that Mrs. Dinwoodie," said Snead.

"They don't come any better," McGonigle agreed. "I'm figuring on getting married to her, if she'll have me."

Snead stared at him.

"After all these years?"

"Why not?"

Snead nodded. "Good question," he said. "Why not? Here we are, out on the road, day in and day out — what do we come back to? You've got the right idea, Skates. More power to you. And good luck."

They shook hands.

"Thanks," said McGonigle.

"I hope you'll be very happy. And for a wedding present I'll tell you what I'm going to do."

"What's that?"

"I'm going to tip you off to a hockey player. A doozer, college boy."

"What's the matter with him?"

"Nothing. He's a doozer."

"And you're telling *me* about him?"

"I wouldn't tell you about him if there was a chance in the world that we could sign him. But we can't. We tried. His old man won't let him, doesn't like us. So just to show you my heart's in the right place I'll give you next chance. Ever hear of Benright College?"

"Benright?" McGonigle thought about it. "Not in Canada."

"No, it's American. The boy is there on a sports scholarship. Comes from a little town in Saskatchewan."

"These American colleges are picking up a lot of good players," agreed McGonigle. "Where's Benright?"

"In Ohio. Benright, Ohio. Slip down there and take a gander at this lad. You'll be interested. His name is Whittaker. Junior year. Write it down."

"Thanks a lot, Blackjack." McGonigle wrote it down in his notebook. The name of Benright College rang a bell, faintly. He had come across it somewhere in a magazine. An advertisement toward the back of the book. It came back to him. He put the notebook away.

"Benright," he said. "That must be quite a hockey team. No campus. No rink."

"Ah!" said Snead. "You've heard of Benright College, then?"

"Correspondence school," said McGonigle. "You get your lessons by mail."

"You're getting too smart for me," said Blackjack Snead.